PUBLISHER/EDITOR
K. Allen Wood

CONTRIBUTING EDITORS
John Boden
Catherine Grant
Barry Lee Dejasu
Zachary C. Parker

COPY EDITOR
Sarah Wood

LAYOUT/DESIGN
K. Allen Wood

COVER DESIGN
Mikio Murakami

Established in 2009
www.shocktotem.com

"Clocks" first appeared in *The Horror Show*,
Phantom Press, 1989

"The Man of Her Dreams" first appeared in
A Dangerous Magic, DAW Books, 1999

"She Cries" first appeared in *Anthology: Year
One*, Four Horsemen LLC, 2012

ISSN 1944-110X

Printed in the United States of America.

Notes from the Editor's Desk

Welcome to the second *Shock Totem* holiday issue!

Love is in the air, my friends. Can you feel it? The most wonderful and diabolical emotion of them all, and we're going to celebrate it. Ostensibly as a Valentine's Day issue, but really...it's all about love.

And horror, of course.

In this special edition of Shock Totem you will find nine short stories and ten anecdotal nonfiction pieces. Up first, Darrell Schweitzer's beautifully tragic "Clocks," one of my favorite short stories, which I am honored to reprint here. "Silence," by Robert J. Duperre, is a gut-wrenching tale of love, war, and death. You won't soon forget this one. Amanda C. Davis's quirky "Omen" was originally written for one of our prompted flash fiction contests, so it's nice to welcome this one home.

In "Broken Beneath the Paperweight of Your Ghosts," Damien Angelica Walters tells of a man and his tattered heart. Catherine Grant's "Sauce" teaches us that sometimes things left behind are best left alone. Tim Waggoner examines the perfect lover in "The Man of Her Dreams." "Hearts of Women, Hearts of Men," by Zachary C. Parker, follows a battered woman struggling to free herself from an abusive relationship while a serial killer is on the loose. This is Parker's debut, and we're very happy to offer it to our readers.

Like our previous holiday issue (Christmas 2011), the fiction is paired with nonfiction, this time by Violet LeVoit, Jassen Bailey, Kristi Petersen Schoonover, C.W. LaSart, Bracken MacLeod, John Dixon, and more. True tales of first loves, failed relationships, misfortune, death, sex, and meatloaf. Trust me, you'll dig it.

Love has its dark side, folks, and fittingly this issue has very sharp teeth.

So there you have it. I'd say I love you, but that'd be weird.

Instead I'll just say thank you. Hope you enjoy what lies ahead.

K. Allen Wood
February 14, 2014

Contents

CLOCKS

by Darrell Schweitzer

He returned to the house again on an evening in November. He had been away a year, but nothing had changed. The house stood pale and dark among the trees as the twilight deepened, as the walls, trees, ground, and sky all faded into that particular autumn grey which is almost blue. He paused in the cold air, listening to the rain hiss faintly on the fallen leaves, wishing he could remain there forever, that time would cease its motion and this moment would never pass.

But, inevitably, as he did every year, he made his way along the leaf-covered path to the front porch. Again he stood procrastinating, fumbling with his keys until his fingers, by themselves, found the key he needed and his hand had turned it in the lock before he was even aware. Then he stepped into the dark house, the door sweeping aside a year's worth of junk mail he had never been able to cancel.

Behind him, the rain whispered, and when he closed the door there was another sound, a faint ticking. He stooped to gather the junk mail into a basket, and noticed the clock on the mail stand, a few inches from his face. It was a cheap, plastic thing, decorated with figures of shepherd girls, like characters out of *Heidi*.

It was one of his wife's clocks. As long as her clocks were here, she was too, in a way. All her life, Edith had collected clocks.

He wound it, and it seemed to tick louder. Then he stood up and wound a row of little golden alarm clocks that stood along the top of a bookcase to his left. They had stopped, and now they added to the faint, rhythmical ticking. He didn't set the time on any of them. That wasn't the point.

It was only after he had completed this task that he turned on the lights, surveyed the hallway, and stepped to his right, into the living room. The ticking followed him, until it was lost in the deeper sound of the grandfather clock that waited in the shadows by the fireplace. He remembered how they had found that grandfather clock in an antique shop once, long, long ago, how Edith had raved over it, begging him to buy it in her joking-but-earnest way, until he relented (even though they *couldn't* afford it). There had been weekends spent polishing, repairing, finishing. In the end, when they were ready, when the thing stood dark and gleaming in the living room, it had been like a birth. Or that was how he remembered it now.

He flicked on one small light, and saw in the semi-darkness another clock humped on the mantle piece. There was a story about that one, too, and as he wound the clock, once more the memory came to him.

Then he sat down by the empty fireplace, exhausted and sad. He put his feet up on a little stool and stared into the fireplace for a while, listening to the clocks. The house was stirring, the soft tick-tick-ticking like the breathing of a great beast turning in its sleep.

He dozed off, and when he awoke it was dark outside. He heard sounds from the kitchen, dishes touching gently, a cabinet door closing, but he remained where he was, listening to those sounds and to the clocks.

The grandfather clock chimed softly.

A few minutes later he did get up, his joints aching. He realized that he was still wearing his hat and coat. He left them on the chair and walked through a narrow hall, past the dark basement stairway, into the kitchen.

There was a steaming cup of tea on the counter by the sink, and two slices of warm toast on a plate, both buttered, one with jam, one without, the way she had always fixed them for him when he worked late at night. He turned and stretched to wind the clock on top of the spice cabinet. It was a smiling metal Buddha with the clock face in its belly, a ridiculous thing (again, full of memories), but she had put it there once, long, long ago, and there it remained, gazing down at him serenely as he ate his toast and drank his tea.

He was almost crying then, but he held back his tears as he went from room to room, winding clocks, until their sound was like that of a million tiny birds outside the windows, gently, very patiently pecking to get in.

Upstairs, a door closed.

In the library he found a brush with

long, blonde hairs in it, discarded on a desktop.

He used a key to wind an intricately carven wooden castle of a clock, where armored knights appeared on the battlements at the ringing of every hour.

The ticking was still gentle, but more insistent, unyielding, like the sound of surf on a quiet night.

When he had made a circuit of the first floor, he came to the front door again, but turned away from it and slowly climbed the front stairs. He was sobbing by then. The sounds from behind him seemed to rise, to propel him up the stairs.

He found his wife's furry slippers at the top, neatly together by the bathroom door where she often left them. He wept, and leaned his head against the wall, pounding softly with his fist.

More than anything else, he wanted just to leave, but then he heard the singing from behind the bedroom door, and he knew that, of course, he could not go away. The song was one he had taught Edith before they were married, long, long ago.

He entered the bedroom and she was there, and she was young and beautiful. She helped him undress and pulled him into the bed, whispering softly as she did, then silent, and for a while he was completely happy, suspended in a single moment of time.

A clock ticked on the night stand.

When he awoke it was morning and she was gone. The empty half of the bed was cold, the covers thrown back. He wept again, bitterly, deeply, cursing himself for having continued the cruel, miraculous farce, for torturing himself one more time, for doing this, somehow, to her, once again. He held up his hands before his face, and he saw how wrinkled the backs of them were, how age-spotted. He touched the top of his head, running his fingers through his thinning hair.

She had still been twenty-six and beautiful. She would always be twenty-six and beautiful.

And the memories came flooding back with horrible vividness, until he was living them again: the rainy night, the screeching tires, the car on its side by the road's edge, Edith in his arms while one set of headlights after another flared by and nobody stopped for what seemed like hours.

He turned over in the bed and pressed his face into the pillow, crying like a small child, and hoping, absurdly, that he would eventually run out of tears.

He tried to tell himself that he wouldn't come again next year, that this would finally cease, but he knew better. When he got up to dress and found a note stuck onto the telephone by the bed, it was only a confirmation.

The note said:

I LOVE YOU
— EDITH.

He was still crying, but softly, as he went down the front stairs, around and into the kitchen, and from there down the dark, creaking stairway into the basement. At the bottom he stood once more, wishing he could remain there motionless forever, that he didn't have to go forward, but, again, he knew better. He flicked on the lights, revealing the thousands upon thousands of clocks that filled the basement, crowded on shelves, standing against the walls, spread across the floor, and holding in their midst by a fantastic spider web of wires a closed coffin that seemed to float a few inches above the rug. It was as if the clocks had grown there, proliferating. He had long since given up wondering if there were more of them now than there had once been.

His mind could supply no explanation, but he knew that somehow, if even one clock in the whole house remained running—and somehow, in defiance of all reason, one or more would always keep running for a whole year, awaiting his return—on this one night in November time would stop, or perhaps slide backwards, and Edith would be as she had been the night before her death, loving him, never aware of any future, forever young while he continued to age. He didn't know if it was real or not. There no longer seemed to be such things as real and unreal.

But he could never, never bring himself to put an end to it, and he wept as he made his way gingerly among the clocks, winding each one. Their voices grew louder and louder, resonating in the cramped basement, while he sobbed and trembled and worked with furious, desperate care, and in the end the sound of them was like screaming.

Darrell Schweitzer's stories have appeared in *Cemetery Dance*, *Night Cry*, *Twilight Zone*, *Interzone*, *The Horror Show*, *Postscripts*, and in numerous anthologies. His novels are *The Mask of the Sorcerer*, *The Shattered Goddess*, and *The White Isle*. He has authored numerous collections, including his latest, *Echoes of the Goddess*, a companion to *The Shattered Goddess*. He has been nominated for the World Fantasy Award four times and won it once, for co-editing *Weird Tales*, something he did for 19 years. He has edited anthologies since: *The Secret History of Vampires*, *Cthulhu's Reign*, *Full Moon City*, and the forthcoming Cthulhu Mythos anthology *That Is Not Dead*.

HOLIDAY RECOLLECTION
LOSE AND LEARN

by Brian Hodge

My first love lasted three years, and straddled high school and college. It ended the way they usually do: with the feeling that all life on earth had been extinguished.

Her name was Susan, and she took what already would've been good years and made them radiant. They also became my first great lesson in the perils of not paying attention to what's going on under the surface. At that age, guys are all pretty much variations on a single theme: hormone-addled lunkhead. We have to learn the hard way.

I never saw the parallels myself, but I reminded Susan of her father. I was also the first guy she'd gone out with that he actually liked. All well and good, I suppose, until her father decided he'd had enough of family life, and bailed on his wife, two daughters, and son. Susan didn't have a lot to say about this, and in my lunkheaded myopia, I just thought she was handling it superbly.

Some months later, she broke things off with me and took up with a guy who was ten years older, and had been hanging around the family via her younger brother. They eventually got married. Not a terribly bright fellow, I don't think; he's the only person I've ever heard of who called someone to ask what night a New Year's Eve party was going to be. But, in retrospect, I have to think he offered a level of security and stability that, at the time, I couldn't. And, of course, he was so very different from her father.

That didn't last but a few years either.

Somewhere in there, a mutual friend told me that Susan had confessed this to her: "I don't know what Brian sees in me. He's so artistic, and I'm so practical." This from a girl who was not only fiercely smart, sweet, and funny, but a wonderful singer, flutist, and pianist. I'd never had a clue she felt that way. Which isn't to say none were there. I'm not sure I would've known what to do with one even if I'd recognized it.

They say you never get over your first love. And maybe we shouldn't. So long as we hang onto the right things.

HEARTS OF WOMEN, HEARTS OF MEN

by Zachary C. Parker

The Camaro's lights flashed twice in rapid succession. *I know you see me. I see you, too.*

Megan had spotted the car in the lot before, but never this close. The diner's broad windows and industrial lighting made her feel both trapped and exposed, an actress thrust upon a stage for the sole amusement of the silhouette behind the steering wheel.

She turned her back on the Camaro and transferred a pair of eggs from the grill to a plate, then added strips of bacon and a sprig of parsley. One of the eggs had ruptured and now resembled an eye dripping down a white cheek. She set the plate in front of a balding man absorbed in the sports section. Being the small operation that *Dale's* was, the waitresses doubled as cooks and busboys, even if their wages didn't account for the extra responsibilities.

It was almost closing time, and aside from a few regulars and a handful of others, the diner was empty. Barb, the other waitress on duty, stood at the edge of a booth, batting her eyelashes and chatting up a group of college boys half her age. Now and then she leaned forward to rap her lacquered nails on the edge of the table and provided a good look at her cleavage. The boys were eating it up.

The one time Megan had tried this routine, she'd been struck with the image of herself replacing Barb, the front of her uniform pulled low to reveal withered and spotted breasts, lunch breaks filled with one lipstick-smeared Pall Mall after another behind the dumpster. The tip had been the largest of the evening, but the encounter had left her feeling dirty, and she'd made sure to spend the money before picking up her son, Jack, from the sitter's.

At the opposite end from the college boys and Barb, a woman with dark hair and a thin face raised a mug to signal for a refill. She wasn't a regular yet, but she had all the marks of one. Megan had seen her twice earlier in the week, ordering coffee and not much else, always paying with change and leaving a few nickels and dimes beyond what she owed.

She'd emptied a box of candy hearts onto her placemat and was busy turning them right-side up, sugary red letters displaying messages of love and other expressions.

"Candy hearts, again?" Megan asked, refilling the woman's mug.

"I like to think of them as antacids," she said. "Helps with the heartburn. Probably all in my head, though." She offered a crestfallen smile that didn't betray any teeth and popped a candy into her mouth. A dull crack issued from inside. In the unforgiving light of the diner, dark circles encroached on the woman's eyes, painting them as cold cherry pits. A thick layer of foundation called attention to the poorly disguised bruise along the right side of her face. The signs of abuse made the candies difficult to stomach, another reason to hate February. Megan wouldn't be surprised if the woman was staying at the battered women's shelter a few blocks over.

"Placebo effect," Megan said.

The woman nodded and blew on her coffee, ripples sputtering across the surface. "Something like that."

The roar of an engine rose from the parking lot, and a pair of headlights flashed to life. The Camaro spun its tires, squealing on the pavement, before it fishtailed and straightened parallel to the front of the diner. For a moment, Megan had a clear view of the man behind the wheel, of David, a scowl on his face that reminded her of the way Travolta had looked in *Carrie*, the image grotesque and ridiculous and outdated. A bottle hurtled through air, arcing end over end to shatter against the window framing the booth. She flinched as a web of cracks radiated from the point of impact. Something was shouted from the Camaro's open window, then the engine revved once more and the car shot off into the nighttime traffic, taillights swallowed by the dark.

The woman gave an appraising look but said nothing, for which Megan was grateful. Instead she popped another heart into her mouth and chased it with coffee.

"Well isn't that wonderful," Barb yelled.

She handed one of the boys a sundae he likely hadn't ordered. "Can't you get through a shift without causing everyone grief?" The boys twisted around in the booth and stared at Megan as she stood in slack surprise.

"Excuse me?" Megan said.

"We never had this kind of trouble until Dale hired you on. You wait until he sees that window." She turned back to the boys, stealing the occasional glance in Megan's direction as she spoke in hushed tones.

Two police cruisers pulled in twenty minutes later, though Megan hadn't heard anyone call them. She'd gone through the motions often enough in the six months since her separation that the questioning seemed a charade. One officer scribbled notes while the other spoke to dispatch between bursts of static. Barb pressed one manicured hand over her heart and repeated over and again how frightened she'd been, hanging on the note taker's arm. Next came the same old words spoken with different voices. *Yes, ma'am, we'll take care of it.* And *yes, ma'am, we deal with this sort of thing all the time.* Then they were gone.

At ten, they turned out the remaining customers and locked the doors. The last of the dishes were cleaned, the tables cleared, the grills scrubbed, and the drawers counted down in silence. As they closed, Megan stole occasional glances out at the lot, now empty except for her beat up Datsun and Barb's pickup. The Camaro didn't return.

Jack was fast asleep when Megan reached the sitter's. She handed over half of the day's tips in exchange for her son and buckled him into the back seat, admiring the tuft of thick black hair protruding from beneath the hood of his coat.

On the drive home, she watched him in the rearview mirror, his head tucked into his chest like a chick trying to keep warm. She also watched for headlights. As each set came into view, she analyzed their size, their brightness, always on the lookout for the particulars. The backstreets were shorter, but she stuck to the main roads when possible. In the weeks since David had started showing up outside the diner, she'd been assailed by dreams of the Datsun stalled at an intersection, headlights filling her vision before several hundred horsepower of American muscle crushed the little car's frame and showered her with glass.

She turned on her blinker and swung into the Shady Oaks apartment complex.

"You smell like pancakes," Jack mumbled, half asleep.

"You smell like a monkey."

A repetitive baseline sounded somewhere in the building, but the stairs and hall were empty, as was their apartment. She'd made a habit of setting Jack just inside the door as she checked over the small one bedroom with her keys laced between her fingers, turning on each light and peering into the closets, under the bed they shared.

"All clear?" Jack asked.

"Yup. No monsters anywhere. Let's get ready for bed. It's late."

"I brushed my teeth at Nina's."

Megan nodded. "Do you think you can brush them again for me?"

"No." Jack crossed his arms, lips extended in a pout.

"If you go brush your teeth and put your pajamas on, we can make up the news before bed. How's that sound?"

She loved to watch him consider things, his face scrunched in concentration while he decided what shirt to wear or whether he wanted the crusts cut from his sandwiches. He weighed everything, examining all the angles.

"Okay," he said, then started for bathroom.

Once they'd washed up and changed, they climbed into bed and turned on the TV for what Jack had dubbed "making up the news." This consisted of Megan turning the TV to the local news and muting the volume so she could silently read the subtitles while the two of them took turns making up their own stories for the newscasters. *Fatal accident on I-90* became *Tyrannosaurus Sighted, Cars Crushed Underfoot.* The latest celebrity drama morphed into *Aliens Invade Hollywood, Wear Too Much Makeup in Poor Attempt at Disguise.*

The eleven o'clock news was well underway when Megan hit mute and enabled the subtitles. A reporter with overly-large teeth and a drab suit jabbered hurriedly into a microphone. Behind him, several cruisers sat parked at the local precinct. A pair of officers passed and disappeared inside. Boxes of text formed above the reporter before disappearing under the weight of new lines.

—*previous three incidents, contents include both a human heart and current driver's license of the presumed*—

"There's a party going on at the police station," Jack said. "It's the police chief's birthday and everyone is invited. They have seven chocolate cakes and two vanilla cakes."

—*too early to confirm the identity of the victim, initial tests match blood type displayed*—

"How old is the chief, Jack?"

"Seventeen million."

"That old, huh?"

"Yeah. They used a dump truck to bring the candles and a flamethrower to light them all." Jack made a *whoosh* sound and swept his arms over the top of the blanket.

—*more information as it becomes available*—

"Sounds dangerous."

"Nope. The firefighters are invited.

Everyone is invited."

A balding weatherman dressed in gray gestured to a cold front overtaking the Midwest, swirls of green clouds falling apart only to reappear and crumble once more. For reasons Megan couldn't understand, Jack always ceased his interpretations during this segment, shushing her if she tried to talk.

The sound of an antique telephone issued from her purse. She'd forgotten to silence her cell. The two of them exchanged glances as the phone rang a second and third time.

"Is it him?" Jack asked.

"Of course not," Megan said. "It's just a wrong number." In her mind's eye she could see David, his forearm draped over the top of yet another payphone, a cigarette burning to the filter between his fingers. And if she picked up the phone, she'd hear nothing but quiet breathing in the space between her ear and the receiver, the same breathing she'd listened to every night for months before she'd worked up the nerve not to answer. The phone went to voicemail, and before the caller could try again, she reached into her purse and set the ringer to silent.

Jack stared at her, his expression close to the one associated with his decision making, only darker.

The news had moved to a woman standing beside the highway. The occasional taillight flickered in the background.

"Looks like another dinosaur sighting," Megan said.

Jack pointed to the tree line behind the highway, the phone call forgotten. "Those trees are perfect for Bigfoot. I bet the reporter will find a million Bigfoot tracks in there."

His words came out so matter-of-factly that she couldn't help but smile. "Yeah, I suppose you're right."

The next morning, Dale pulled Megan into his office, which was nothing more than a massive desk crammed into a nook beside the walk-in freezer, and asked about the events of the previous night. When Dale had interviewed her, she'd said nothing of David or her pending divorce, and when faced with her new boss's inquiries and offers for help, she still clung to the idea that she could have a fresh start, that she could be something other than the center of attention. And so it was with this hope that she brushed his questions aside with apologies and promises that there would be no further incidents.

Aside from the occasional glare from Barb and the usual chaos of the breakfast rush, the morning was blissfully uneventful. Kate, another recent hire who had a boy around Jack's age, helped break the mood with pinches of dialogue between taking orders and refilling coffee. Every now and then the two of them would look to the shattered window and then to each other, making exaggerated frowns that lightened the mood more than Megan had thought possible.

It wasn't until noon that the Camaro appeared, David's stark, black hair, gray eyes, and pinched nose clearly visible in the light of day. He was eating a hamburger. A paper sack sat on the dash, and now and then he would reach inside for a handful of fries. Ketchup dotted the front of his blue coveralls. Apparently he'd decided to spend his lunch break outside the diner rather than at the garage. Or perhaps the police had gone there looking for him.

If he was on his lunch break, he'd be gone within the hour. Still, she hated the idea of going about her job while he watched undisturbed. Another part of her, the part that yearned to dissolve into anonymity, liked the idea of bringing a few police cruisers into the parking lot for the lunch crowd to gawk at even less. With steady, measured steps, she rounded the counter, took the phone from the wall, and punched in three numbers at random. Outside, David straightened in his seat.

She tried to think how many times an emergency call might ring and after a moment fed details into the receiver, mouthing the words *husband* and *violation* and *restraining order*. Halfway through reciting the diner's address, the Camaro cranked to life and disappeared into traffic.

She hung up the phone and leaned back against the counter. The clink of forks and knives and the drone of the jukebox seemed diminished, as if wrapped in layer upon layer of plastic. Somewhere behind her, a customer called for an extra set of silverware, and when the request was not honored, called more loudly. It was a long time before Megan could reply and even longer before her shaking legs could support her.

When two o'clock rolled around, she punched her time card, climbed behind the wheel of the Datsun, and set off to pick up some groceries before the elementary school let out.

On her way to the Dollar Mart, she took the route leading past St. Julian's, the battered women's shelter a few blocks from the diner. Old Victorian houses with wraparound porches and all manner of windows slumbered on each side of the street. Several of these houses, including the women's shelter, had been converted into something new. A bed and breakfast. A funeral home. A consignment shop.

The shelter loomed ahead on her right. The massive brick structure gave a sense of security and stability. White shutters and a wide front porch softened the otherwise hard appearance. In what she now thought of as the Bad Days, back when she and David still lived together, she would drive down this street three or four times a week for no other reason than to look at the house and the women who sometimes sat on the porch in the evenings. Even now she wondered if she and Jack might not end up there still.

She scanned the porch for any sign of the customer with the bruised cheek and candy hearts as she passed. Had the woman had long hair? Short? Blue or brown eyes? She tried to conjure the woman's face only to be met with a bruised and tired abstraction. In any case, the porch sat empty.

The radio promised record snowfall throughout the night and into the next day, and by the time she pulled into the Wright Elementary bus loop with a few modest bags of groceries the storm was underway.

Jack clambered into the backseat and fastened his seatbelt.

"How was school?"

"Ben and Cory said we're going to have a snow day tomorrow!"

"Not if I send you out with a shovel."

"Can I stay up late and watch the weather?"

Megan laughed. Other kids were already making plans for snow forts and her son was excited to watch the weather. "We'll see if they announce a delay."

"Okay."

"Guess what I'm making for dinner."

"Pizza?"

"Nope."

"Macaroni and cheese with breadcrumbs?" In her son's world, there were two types of mac and cheese. One came from a box, the other had breadcrumbs.

"With breadcrumbs," Megan said.

"Awesome."

That night they cooked dinner together. Megan poured the contents of a mixing bowl into a casserole dish and smoothed them with the backside of a spoon while Jack followed behind with measured sprinkles of crumbs. The two played Go Fish and War at the table while their meal cooked and cooled, then retreated to the bedroom with a bowl each to make up the news.

They tuned in to the continued search for Bigfoot, which was losing steam as the snow rolled in due to a shortage of snowshoes. Jack explained all of this around a mouthful of macaroni, fork clattering in his bowl all the while. Next came mutant basketball players hired to test anti-gravity boots, then Jack's beloved weatherman. Waves of shimmering greens and blues washed over the screen as the man gestured excitedly.

"I want to make up the weather when I grow up," Jack said after the report was over. A commercial for deodorant filled the screen.

"You'll make a great weatherman." Megan ruffled his hair.

When the commercials ended, a view of the police station appeared. The reporter from the previous night stood with his collar popped against the wind, microphone clutched to his chest. Behind him, a crowd gathered at the station doors.

—*We have just received word that remains belonging to the fifth victim of what authorities are now calling the Mason Jar Killer have been*—

"There's a monster on the loose," Jack

said.

"What?" His words were so close to the mark that for a moment she'd forgotten the game. "Oh, Bigfoot. Right."

"No." Jack shook head. "This is something mad. It wants to tear people into little pieces."

Megan jabbed a button on the remote. The screen went black. "That isn't a nice thing to say, Jack. I don't like that very much."

He shrugged his shoulders and pushed the remnants of his macaroni around the bottom of his bowl. "Sorry."

"Let's not make up stories like that in the future, okay? Finished?"

"Yes." Jack speared the last of the macaroni and handed over his bowl.

"I think we're all a little tired. Let's get ready for bed, huh?"

As Jack showered, Megan washed the dishes and wrapped up the leftovers from the casserole dish, her son's words echoing in her head. This was the kind of thing that made her mute the news in the first place, so much of it a constant stream of negativity. She didn't want to smother him, but she didn't want him exposed either.

She placed the mixing bowl in the sink. The dark thoughts came. David putting holes in the drywall. Jack huddled in his room. A wrench coming down on her knee, her shoulder, her thigh. And then screaming. Always screaming.

To Jack's delight, school was cancelled. The temperature had fallen drastically in the night and several inches of snow coated the world outside their windows. Much of the day was spent in the same manner as the previous night, the two of them playing cards and watching TV in bed. After a lunch of leftover macaroni, Megan dressed for work and bundled Jack for the ride to the Nina's. It took a full five minutes to clear the Datsun of snow and another five for it to heat while they waited inside the stairwell. Only when she took out her phone to check the time did she realize she'd received no phantom calls in the night.

"Well, that's a first."

"What is?" Jack asked.

"Nothing. What do you think about this weather?"

"I can see why the weatherman was excited."

Megan stomped her boots on the welcome mat and gave the diner's door a stern tug, securing it against the wind. Kate stood behind the counter.

"I thought Barb worked the closing shift?" Megan said.

"Called off. Says she's snowed in."

"Snowed in? She's the only one of us with four-wheel drive." Megan deposited her coat and hat in the break room.

"I told Dale I'd cover her shift so you wouldn't have to close alone. He said to stay open until they upgrade the snow emergency to level three."

"How much business does he think we're going to get?" She scanned the booths and the row of stools lined up at the counter, all of which were empty. "Have you even had any customers?"

"A few." Kate's phone chirped in her pocket, and she pulled it out to examine a text. "At any rate, I don't think we'll be open for long."

Megan nodded.

"My neighbor," Kate said, slipping her phone back into her pocket. "She's watching Randall."

For the next hour, they talked amongst themselves and tried to keep busy, discussing the storm and Barb and Dale and the men who frequented the diner, but mostly their children. As it turned out, Randall also attended Wright, though he was a grade ahead of Jack. Megan wiped down the tables and vacuumed while Kate restocked the various dispensers and scrubbed the hard to reach parts of the grills. After a time, they took a break to fry themselves eggs and a few strips of bacon. The weather report cut in and out of the little radio Kate had moved out of the break room. Now and then Megan looked to the fractured window and the heavy snowfall beyond, but each look conjured images of David parked behind the diner, prepared to run her down the moment she set foot outside, and so she kept busy and tried to put the window out of her mind.

"Dammit," Kate said. She had her phone out again.

"What's up?"

"Randall. He threw up all over my neighbor's couch. She can't get him to stop crying."

Megan nibbled on the last of the bacon and watched Kate launch into a series of replies, thumbs flitting across her worn out flip phone. She took out her own phone and checked the screen. No messages. No emergencies from her own sitter.

"Go on," she heard herself say, the words sounding very far away. "This place is dead, anyway. I can finish up by myself."

"What? No, I'm sure he'll be okay," Kate said, but there was worry in her voice. "I couldn't just leave you here."

"If it was Jack, I know I'd want to go."

Kate chewed her lower lip, seeming to consider the option. "You're sure?"

Megan nodded. She tried not to look at the shattered window.

"Thank you." Kate disappeared into the

break room and returned a moment later with her coat. "Stay warm and drive safe. Thanks again." Kate pushed through the doors and was gone.

"Shit." Megan looked over the rows of vacant booths. She'd known the diner would close early, that business would be slow and the tips wouldn't cover the cost of leaving Jack with the babysitter, but she'd never been one to shirk her responsibilities. Now a new set of concerns overtook her financial woes, concerns involving response times and isolation and whether winter tires were included in the budget for the police force.

She locked the door and returned to the counter. She'd stay open, but anyone desperate enough for pancakes or coffee would have to knock. A gust of wind rattled the windows and made the diner's ancient ceiling creak. Halfway down the line of windows, the spider web of cracks inflicted by the bottle stood illuminated in frost. Megan shivered.

By the time the snow emergency was upgraded, it was after nine and the streets were dead. There had been no customers, and in the last few hours she'd seen nothing but plows on the strip. Across the road, a gas station and fast food restaurant had gone dark. The world was white and empty.

She switched off the radio and listened to the wind howl against the sides of the diner. Would she be able to hear an engine idling over the storm? She didn't know. She fished her cellphone from her pocket and considered calling the police now that Dale wasn't around. But for what? To escort her to the Datsun less than twenty feet from the door? She returned the phone to her pocket and pulled the zipper of her coat to her chin.

When she finally set foot outside, panic seized her in a wave. All at once, the wind carried with it the roar of engines and screams and curses and other nightmarish sounds, and the snow was a fog through which the her worst fears appeared and dissolved like the clouds of color on the weather segment of the news. Her breath caught in her throat, and she slipped in her dash for the car, hip smacking the ice and snow with force. Crawling. Scrambling. Sprinting once again. *One more limp to hide. One more bruise to cover*. She hit the door and tugged the handle ineffectually as snow slid from the roof and widow and down her coat, fresh tears freezing to her face in the process until she remembered the keys clutched in her numb fingers.

She collapsed in the driver's seat and took gaping breaths and sobbed until her lungs could offer a frustrated scream. The overhead light cast jerking shadows as she brought her hands down on the wheel, and the horn blared under their combined weight. She fumbled along the door until her fingers found the lock and pushed. She'd made it.

The snow on the driver side window had been knocked loose during her struggle with the door, and through it she could see the empty parking lot and diner. No Camaro. No David. She leaned back and tried to breathe. Only then did she notice the thing on the passenger seat.

It was a Mason jar, like the ones her mother had used to preserve peaches, only bigger, perhaps the biggest she'd seen, though much of it was empty. At a glance it looked as though the jar contained some strange red fruit, slick and nestled in a bed of snow with something like a library card tucked beside it. As she leaned closer, the contents redefined themselves. A human heart half covered in large salt crystals, the kind with which one might salt a sidewalk, filled the center. Much of the salt had gone pink in color, and a thin layer of blood had pooled at the bottom of the jar.

Megan covered her mouth and turned the jar until the face on what was an Ohio driver's license was visible. The dark hair, the pinched nose. Even with the streak of dark red over the photo, she'd recognize the man anywhere.

A second wave of panic threatened to overwhelm her as she fumbled out her phone and guided a shaking finger toward those three digits every member of society knows. She pressed the first two and stopped. Perched on the dashboard in plain view was a box of candy hearts.

Slowly and deliberately, she closed the phone and slid it back into her pocket. The box looked fresh, unopened. Atop the box sat a solitary blue heart. Five sugary red letters faced upward—SMILE.

Zachary C. Parker is a recent graduate of Bowling Green State University. He is currently serving as an editor at Shock Totem Publications and writing freelance in the game industry. In his free time he reads, murders people living inside his word processor, and tests the grandfather paradox with the time machine in his closet. To find out more, visit his crucially underdeveloped blog at wordsbytorchlight.com.

HOLIDAY RECOLLECTION
UNLEARNING TO LIE
by Mason Bundschuh

She was fierce and wild, all summer-tanned and smelling of honey and mystery, and I was stupid enough to love her. I should have known—no, I knew; even then I knew, for she always went quiet when I pressed my earnest and awkward love. But that is what we do when we are young, tumble headlong against all caution.

It took her months to break the silence; that was when I learned to lie about matters of love.

She asked if it broke my heart that she didn't love me. Then and only then did I truly see her and not the fabricated icon I'd venerated all those months.

No, no. It's okay.

I'm sure she didn't believe me. I don't think I meant for her to. Such are the little knife twists of love. But she was polite and did not call my bluff.

"It's okay," I said, "I understand."

But I didn't understand. I didn't, even when she married my best friend and asked me to play a song at their wedding. Even when her children appeared, and life moved on, and I forgot how her hair smelled and the particular electric color of her eyes. And not when I got the call that her husband left her for another man's wife.

One part of me (the foolish part that shames me every day) thought, *If you had picked me.* But then in a rush came a memory, hidden under scarred self-loathing, of a time long after that wasted summer when I didn't tell the truth and lied to a girl who asked if I loved her.

Those lies you can't take back. Too late I understand.

Sauce

by Catherine Grant

Bill stared at the last plastic container of Tawny's marinara sauce in the freezer. He wanted the sauce more than a cold beer on Super Bowl Sunday, but he knew that if he ate it today, it would be the last vision of Tawny he would ever have. Unless she came back to him, of course. It was a hope that had once burned so deep, but after three months that red hot optimism had faded into cold, gunmetal gray.

When Tawny left him, swearing at him in patois as she packed her bags, her big brown eyes afire with anger, she was at an end, a woman broken, who could not be put back together, especially by Bill's careless hands. Now, there was nothing left of her in the apartment save for ghosts of perfume on the bedsheets and a drawer in the bathroom full of mysterious toiletries that he hadn't been able to throw away.

He'd spent the first month coming home to an empty, dark house, which had once been full of light and spices and the deep magic of meals prepared by delicate hands. After six weeks of takeout and fast food, Bill had opened the freezer and found the plastic containers full of chunky marinara sauce. He thawed one in the microwave and boiled a pot of spaghetti. Tawny had been an excellent cook, but her spaghetti sauce was the stuff of legend, a smooth, thick tomato puree with the right hints of garlic, onion, and even a bit of saffron. Bill poured it over the cooked pasta and drooled a bit onto his chin as he carried the plate to the living room.

The first bite was heaven, a symphony of herbs and oil and tomato in his mouth.

The second bite went deeper. The flavors were earthy, pronounced, even a bit too strong.

With the third bite, Bill gasped as his vision clouded and he felt as if he were falling, dropping into a darkness that was as blue and dark as an ocean at midnight. He tried to catch himself, grab onto something, but his fingers found no purchase.

The ground, concrete, jolted him. Bill lay on a boardwalk, near the ocean. It was night, and the air smelled of brine and bonfire. He stood, looked out across the sand dunes and down to the shore. A large group of people were near the water, drinking beer and laughing. They looked like college students, dressed casually in hoodies, denim, and cotton, stunning in their youth. One of them took out a guitar, and as he strummed a tune, some of the others began to dance, twirling and stumbling in the firelight.

Two of the figures sat apart from the others, near the fire on a piece of driftwood. Their talk was soft, full of smiles and light touches, as they stared into each other's eyes. Bill recognized the younger version of himself, pale and too skinny with a bad haircut. Then his eyes rested on Tawny, and she was exquisite as always. Her curly black hair swayed in the light breeze and she wore a simple cotton dress that accentuated her every curve. Her brown skin like burnished copper in the firelight.

Bill remembered that night. He'd kept looking at her smooth, full mouth, wondering if her kiss would taste like honey. Later, when they'd shared that kiss, it had tasted like sweetness. His fingers lightly trailing the curve of her face and down her neck, her hands on his hips, an anchor among turbulent waters of desire. Bill watched as his memories unfolded in front of his eyes...

When he awoke from the vision, he was on the couch, staring at the ceiling. The remains of Tawny's sauce were on the floor, soaking into the carpet. Bill reached out with a shaking hand, dipped his finger, and then licked the sauce from it. The marinara was lukewarm and delicious, but the vision didn't return. Not even after he scooped two more mouthfuls, hoping with each swallow that he'd be flung back into the dark blue deep, to the bonfire and beach. Bill sighed in resignation. He cleaned the mess, poorly, leaving a streak of red on the beige piling, and went to bed.

Under the covers, he tossed and turned, smelling the occasional puff of Tawny's sandalwood perfume. He dreamed, of her lips dripping with honey, her smooth, hot skin the color of copper. He woke hard and throbbing in the morning, his desire for the woman who had once shared his bed a painful weight on his groin.

✦

The next week, Bill took out another container of sauce before he left for work in the morning. When he arrived home, the sauce on the counter beckoned. He cooked the spaghetti in haste, al dente, and ate ravenously. On the third bite, he tasted the earthiness; and on the fifth, he fell back into the water of his memories with a jolting splash.

The beach was gone. Instead, he was at a party at the local American Legion hall. It was the first birthday party anyone had ever thrown him—his thirtieth. His parents were bad at celebrating anything with enthusiasm, and Bill hadn't so much as received a cake since he was ten, maybe younger. Tawny scheduled a surprise party with all of his friends and family and made jerk chicken and rice and peas, with an artful skill that impressed everyone into silence when the food was served, including Bill.

He watched his pastself open the door and walk into the hall, then look up in slack-jawed wonder. The room was decorated with white lights and Chinese paper lanterns, and the roar of "Surprise!" from his loved ones was deafening. Then Tawny was there, smiling warmly and wrapping her arms around him. She kissed him on the cheek and whispered into his ear: "For this, I want you tonight."

He smiled and kissed her. The onslaught of friends and family came rushing to wish him a happy birthday, smiling and greeting them both in a flood of affection and well-wishes. His best friend gave Tawny the biggest hug of all, telling her that she was good for Bill, that they were good together. She smiled wide and hugged him back.

Everyone ate and danced until late in the evening. Bill drank far too much, and by the time he stumbled into the apartment with Tawny, he was too drunk to perform. He took off his clothes and she tolerated his sloppy, whiskey-soaked kisses until he passed out on top of her, drooling onto her shoulder and pinning her to the bed with his weight.

The memories kept coming, and Old Bill watched as Tawny sighed and pushed him off with some effort. She put her T-shirt and underwear back on in several fluid motions and lay on the very edge of the bed, her back turned to the naked, snoring man sprawled beside her. In the dim street light filtering through the windows, she cried softly.

In the morning, Tawny made him eggs and toast to still his aching stomach. They ate in silence, her face a mask through it all. When he was done, Bill left his plate on the table and kissed her forehead before heading out. Tawny washed dishes, her shoulders slumping as her thoughts seemed to wander. When she'd finished washing the last plate, she turned around to the empty kitchen. A single tear fell down her cheek.

In his logical mind, Bill knew all of this was just a vision, a shade of the past, but he could have sworn she saw him. Looking into her eyes, he felt tightness in his chest. Her emotions flooded him in waves, sadness laced with disappointment and seeds of loneliness that burrowed into the dry, cracked earth of his own heart. The pounding in his chest became irregular, faster, harder.

Bill jolted awake. He stumbled, dizzy and sweating, to the bathroom and retched, gasping as the precious sauce flowed into the water like pureed pink construction paper, the discarded Valentine's Day project of some child who tried to make papier-mâché. Bill flushed it all, willing the visions away.

He went to bed.

He did not dream of honeyed lips

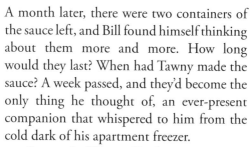

A month later, there were two containers of the sauce left, and Bill found himself thinking about them more and more. How long would they last? When had Tawny made the sauce? A week passed, and they'd become the only thing he thought of, an ever-present companion that whispered to him from the cold dark of his apartment freezer.

Just eat it. What will it hurt?

Indeed, who was really hurt by a little marinara sauce? That night, Bill arrived home from work and couldn't take the temptation any longer. Opening the freezer was barely a consideration. He grabbed one of the two remaining plastic containers, and popped it in the microwave. He didn't bother to boil pasta. When it was heated, he grabbed a spoon and ate the sauce in dripping, heaping mouthfuls.

After the seventh bite, he drifted away.

It was Christmas, two years ago. They were with Tawny's family, her mother and two brothers, both of whom could stand Bill only enough to be barely civil. He told Tawny they felt that way because he was white, but really, Bill knew that was a cop-out. They didn't like him because, in his presence, Tawny seemed to shrink. Instead of being a tall, outspoken empress, she would become a quiet, obedient sidekick to Bill's self-important diatribes about politics or sports. The evening wasn't going well, and when one of Tawny's brothers got up and walked away from the table, Bill only smirked.

Later, at the apartment, Bill and Tawny lay in bed. He took up too much space but he didn't touch her. Tawny didn't seem to care. She'd grown used to his infrequent affection. She turned her head and looked at him, her brown eyes wet pools that reflected the moonlight.

"Why do you have to egg them on?" she whispered. "Can't you just not talk about those things? For me?"

Bill only rolled his eyes and turned his back to her. Long after he drifted off to sleep, Tawny lay there, staring at the ceiling. With a tongue that knew no honey, she licked her dry lips.

Old Bill watched and felt the waves of emotion returning to him, her sorrow feeding the garden that she'd planted on his previous visit to this dream world of memories. He felt the garden grow, sprouting vines and dark saffron-colored flowers that smelled of sandalwood and hickory bonfire. The dry earth of Bill's heart cracked further, the fissures spreading out toward the edges.

He woke up sweating and shaken, but didn't vomit again. Bill got out of bed and went to the kitchen in the dark, knowing the way by memory. He took out the last plastic container and went to the trash, lifting the lid. There, he stopped, his hand hovering over the empty space.

He couldn't throw it out.

Bill cursed at himself. He held the sauce

in his hand and went to the sink. He pried off the plastic lid in a spray of frost and went to turn on the water. He stopped again, his hand hovering over the faucet. He swore he felt one of the fissures in his heart garden snap open further, but even that wouldn't force him to ruin the last bit of Tawny's sauce. His chest burned, and he whimpered, returned the container to the freezer, and went back to bed.

Bill's dreams were violent but quickly faded in the morning. Still, once out of bed, he could only shuffle himself from one room to the next. Even lifting his toothbrush felt like effort. His complexion pallid, the circles under his eyes like bruises. At the office, his boss took one look at him and ordered him to a doctor—or, at the very least, home to bed. Bill chose to take the latter option, and when he got home he fell into his covers and drifted to sleep without undressing.

Upon waking, the first thing that registered was hunger. His stomach uttered a low, savage grumble. He groaned and rubbed his eyes, feeling the ache in his joints from sleeping in the same spot for too long. The burning in his chest had not subsided. It was worse.

In need of food and drink, his body still weak and hot, he opened the refrigerator. The sterile glare of white plastic and a jar of mayonnaise was all he saw. On the bottom shelf sat a week-old burrito. He considered it for a moment, then stood and opened the freezer.

That last container of sauce. He wanted it. More than the breath of life, he needed it—to drown his fever like medicine. Not for the first time he wondered if the sauce was indeed some sort of voodoo. His stomach uttered another savage growl. Bill removed the container and placed it in the microwave to thaw. This time, when it was ready to eat, he didn't bother with a spoon. He bent the plastic back and poured the sauce into his mouth. It was hot and burned his lips, but he didn't care. He continued to pour...

The vision was different this time. It was like being thrown into a pool full of ice water. His heart hammered in his chest. Fast. Too fast. He grimaced as pain shot down his arm. He looked around. He stood in a field that stretched from horizon to horizon, which he didn't remember but was strangely familiar. In the center of the field sat a brown house, sorely neglected and ramshackle. The siding was missing in spots and the windows were broken on the first floor. Bill approached, and he saw that the roof was sunken in on one side.

In the back yard, a marble statue stood immaculate, surrounded by fountains. The rest of the yard was overgrown. Bill recognized the subject of the statue. It was Tawny, sculpted to look like a West Indian goddess. She stared down at him from the pedestal with empty eyes and an expression that saddened him.

In a sudden wind, the back door of the house whipped open and crashed against the siding. Leaving the statue behind, Bill went to the door and stepped inside, out of the fierce gale. The interior of the house was just as ill-kept as the exterior. The furniture moldy and moth-eaten, the floors covered in dust and scraps of rolling paper, the kitchen piled with dishes that smelled of rotten food. As he explored the ground floor, he took it all in, disgusted. He went upstairs, and was greeted by more of the same: a filthy, grime-covered bathroom and bedrooms full of stained sheets and broken appliances.

At the end of the hall, remained one last door, standing out from the others. The wood was a bit brighter, here, clear sky amidst the dark clouds of a storm. He turned the cool doorknob, pushed open the door, and stepped inside.

In one corner of the room sat a queen-sized bed, covered in silk sheets that were neatly folded. In another was a desk piled high with Bill and Tawny's favorite books and her computer. Bill could see that the screen showed a website that sold Tawny's jewelry, a hobby that she'd wanted to turn into a business for as long as he could remember. In another corner was a nursery, empty but clean and new. One of Bill's childhood stuffed animals sat in the corner, a dog he'd named Pongo, which he hadn't seen since he was nine.

Tawny sat on a stool in the middle of it all, lovingly gazing at all the items in the room. Her eyes settled on Bill. "Hello there," she said.

Bill started. "Are you actually...talking to me?"

Tawny smiled and stood, her mane of curls bouncing upon her shoulders. She was wearing her favorite dress, a purple cotton strapless that complimented her skin tone. She'd never looked lovelier, and Bill had the desire to reach out for her, to take her to the bed in the corner and make love.

"You can't do that, Bill," she whispered.

He flinched at the sound of an answer to his unspoken thoughts, but remained silent.

Tawny frowned and approached him. "This place doesn't exist. This house is the life that we could have had, that we should have built together, but that I had to make alone. I could only stay in this room for so long, polishing and preparing to spread out to the other rooms, and then I had to get out." She looked toward each item, the desk, the bed, the empty cradle, and then back to Bill, waiting for a confirmation that he'd heard her. He only stared, his mouth agape.

Tawny pursed her lips and shook her head. She looked into his eyes. "You can leave now, Bill. This is over."

The room faded as Bill opened his mouth to beg her not to go, to stay with him, but his words caught in his throat. The cradle shriveled and then dissolved into powder and shavings. The desk did the same, and the laptop disintegrated into tiny fragments on the floor. The bed sheets melted into a pool of liquid. A crack opened up in the floor, and then the foundation of the house shook. Bill ran, leaving Tawny behind, down the hallway and to the stairs. His feet slipped and he tumbled downward, feeling wood and paint flake away beneath his body. At the bottom landing, he scrambled to his feet and sprinted toward the door, which broke apart like sawdust as he stumbled into the back yard. He found himself standing in front of the statue once again, and when he looked back the house was a pile of rubble. Somewhere in the midst of that ruin were the remains of the life he could have lived, if he'd simply reached out and taken hold of it.

He looked up to the statue. The eyes were no longer lifeless; they were pools of brown flame. The statue moved, and then hopped off the pedestal in one fluid motion. Goddess Tawny looked down at him, her expression pained.

"Goodbye, Bill," she whispered, then walked into the field toward the sunset. She did not look back.

Bill sat on the ground near the fountain and cried. They were the first real tears he'd let out since Tawny left him. When she had packed her bag three months ago, all he'd done was mutter that she should stay, that she was throwing away almost ten years, and then bitterness and anger consumed him.

Now, curled up on the ground, he wept, and his tears watered the garden of his heart. The dark saffron flowers grew too large and the vines burrowed deep into the soil. Bill felt a lance of pain in his chest that became unbearable. He buried his face in the crook of his arm and bit down until he felt blood on his lips. He tasted tomato and garlic. As he clutched and scratched at the remains of his broken heart, Bill's cries turned to choked screams.

Catherine Grant lives in Providence, Rhode Island. She is an Assignment Editor for Shock Totem Publications, office monkey, freelance journalist, bibliophile, gamer and connoisseur of caffeine-laden beverages.

Holiday Recollection
SOMETHING TO CHEW ON
by Kristi Petersen Schoonover

As a kid, Valentine's Day was much anticipated. At school, there were cupcakes and card exchanges; at home, there was Chinese take-out and candy from Mom and Dad. And in 1980, there was a party.

This wasn't any party. My parents were insanely active in our local United Methodist church. Among other things, my mother directed the choir, in which my father sang bass. The choir was at the core of my family's social life, and being part of it was a rite of passage.

Every Thursday, Mom and Dad would go to rehearsal and leave the four of us with a babysitter. I was nine—old enough, in my opinion, to sing with the adults. I was a stubborn, difficult child, and the relationship between me and my parents is best described as a "constant battle of wills" more than anything else, so I was persistent about asking to go. Even though my mother had refused my request several times, that year Valentine's Day fell on a Thursday. Since she'd decided on a short rehearsal followed by a dessert party, she relented and said I could go.

Ecstatic, I planned to wear my favorite dress and from then until the big day helped her make all manner of sweets. I couldn't wait.

At last, February 14 arrived. But things were odd the second I got home from school.

Our candy and gifts—usually concealed until post-chow mein—were displayed on the dining room table, and the smell of cooked meat thickened the air. My aproned mother opened the oven and peered inside at the only meal I despised more than liver and onions: meatloaf.

"What about the Chinese food?" I asked.

She closed the oven door. "We don't have time for that this year. Babysitter's coming at six and we need to be fed and ready to go."

"I hate meatloaf."

"Too bad." She tossed her oven mitt on the counter. "Set the table."

Mom put the brown mass the size of a small brick on my plate. I ate the rice, nearly finished the green beans, and struggled through a few carrots.

Dad eyed me. "We have to get going and you haven't touched your meatloaf."

"I ate almost everything else."

"Eat it."

"But—"

"Your mother is letting you go with us tonight and this is how you repay her? Eat it."

I took a bite. It was like chewing dirty socks.

I knew there was no way I could eat it; I reached for my napkin.

"You will not spit it out. Your mother made it. You will eat it."

"It's disgusting," I said.

My father's face reddened. "Then put other food in with it."

I sipped my water. I forked in a few green beans. Desperate, I added some carrots.

"Swallow it," Dad said.

I shook my head.

"You will swallow that or we'll leave you home."

No. Anything but that! I struggled to

swallow, choked it back up.

"Itssshhh too big!"

"Drink more water."

"Let me shhhpit it out!"

"No." Dad pointed with his fork. "That's it. You're staying home tonight."

I started to cry. I looked to the other kids, but all three of them were focused on playing with their food.

"Stop crying! We tried to give you a privilege and this is how you act. It's quite obvious you don't deserve it."

I looked to my mother for help, but her quiescence made it clear that I was on my own.

The kids finished their dinners and scattered. Mom and Dad prepared to leave. I sat at the table, alone, with the foul lump in my mouth and even more of the wretched stuff on my plate. Pam, the babysitter, was given strict instructions—I was not allowed to spit it out. But I believed that they weren't going to go without me. That they'd change their minds. That I'd still get to don my favorite dress and go to the party.

Until I heard their car pull out of the

driveway.

Silence

by Robert J. Duperre

The demon is in the room with him, and David Higgins knows its name.

It has haunted him for more than forty years, this beast, skulking in the corner of his vision, always lurking, always waiting for its time to strike, its stinking, fetid breath wafting across his nostrils on even the most windless of days. Yet for four decades David has been able to hold it at bay, quashing its advances at every turn. For a long while he thought he had defeated it completely, for in the calm moments in the dark of night, as he lay in his bed sweating while the machine beside him went *ping*, he felt nothing. No fear, no regret, no anger, no anything. And yet here it is again after so long, prowling the outskirts of his living room, goading him, taunting him, promising death. It lingers in the darkness of the doorway, boring deep into his soul.

Of course it would come for me now, he thinks.

David cannot move, cannot defend himself. He is trapped in his living room, strapped into his goddamn wheelchair. ALS has robbed him of motion. Now his eyes are all that move; they swish in their sockets as he points them beyond the doorway. He wishes his daughter Natalie was in here with him. David can hear water running and dishes clanking in the kitchen, as well as a pair of busily chatting voices. Even though she's never even known it existed, Natalie always seems able to cast the evil thing aside, as if her soul itself is made from some sort of ethereal armor. She's been his caretaker ever since the disease began its hateful warping of his body. He yearns to call out to her, but his vocal chords are just as useless as the rest of him.

The machine beside him pings.

David's heart rate is rising.

Low, malicious laughter echoes in his ears. The beast is on the move. His eyes track the black shape as it scuttles across the wall, a living inkblot, barely noticeable in the dim room. The thing moves like a worm, expanding and contracting, gliding over layers of beige paint until it disappears behind the entertainment center. The television clicks on, the ancient picture tube buzzing as the screen begins to glow. The sound grates on him, makes his panic rise. Why couldn't his affliction have robbed him of his hearing, if only to make this one moment more tolerable?

Images appear on the television while to his right the machine goes *ping* once more. *No*, David thinks, but cannot say. *Please, no.* On the screen, Rod Serling takes shape, looking at David from beneath his brow. The theme song rises in volume; *da-na-na-na, da-na-na-na*. Phantom Rod's lips begin to move, ready to impart a nugget of wisdom about the grand irony of life, but David can barely make out the words. *Why isn't Natalie coming to check on me?* he wonders. Televisions don't usually come on all by themselves. It should have caught her attention.

The demon reaches out for him with invisible feelers. His mind starts swimming backward.

This is wrong. I don't want to see.

But the demon doesn't listen.

It is persistent.

And, David now realizes, it is *desperate*.

※

To thirteen-year-old David Higgins, Miss Margery's droning voice was a lot like static. He knew the sound well, since there were many nights when he'd fallen asleep in the den with the television on while watching Twilight Zone *marathons. And just like static, her voice made him want to stay asleep.*

But he couldn't do that. He couldn't close his eyes, nor pay attention to the symbols Miss Margery was scribbling on the blackboard. He couldn't even look at the posters of the Beatles on the wall—like David, Miss Margery was obsessed with them, making sure to tell her class that one day they'd take America by storm—and imagine himself standing on stage alongside Paul and John and George. Nothing mattered, not addition or subtraction or any other boring 6th-grade nonsense. All that did matter was the new kid. Max. The one sitting right in front of him; the one whose hair was sandy-blond and who had a triangle of freckles dotting the back of his neck.

Goose pimples rose on David's arms, and he shivered. Involuntarily, his foot kicked out, clanking against the boy's chair. Max turned, his light blue eyes half-mast as he stared. The left side of the boy's plump lips rose into a half-smile.

"S-sorry," David stammered.

Max swept a stray lock of hair from his brow. "No problem," he whispered with a grin, and turned back around.

David let out a long sigh of relief, then felt instantly afraid that someone might notice. He glanced left and right. Everyone's attention was still on the front of the classroom. Good. He closed his eyes, and in the darkness behind his eyelids, an image of Max took shape. An odd sensation churned in David's stomach.

What he felt scared him. David wasn't what one would call a shy kid, but he was indeed strange, and he knew it. He felt lonely, out of place. When other boys talked of girls, saying words like titties and bush and spanking it, he willingly laughed along. When they showed him dirty pictures, he dutifully looked and whistled. In truth he couldn't understand his classmates' fascination. To him, girls were just like anyone else—friends and neighbors, and nothing more. His interactions with them were never special, and thoughts of their naughty bits only made him feel disgusted. The only erections he ever remembered having were those that made him groan and slide out of bed hunched over in the morning before waddling down the hall for the day's most painful piss.

Yet now here he was, in class of all places, and the thought of Max's face caused him to stiffen. David stifled a groan and shifted uncomfortably in his chair, squeezing his fists as tightly as he could, trying to wish the erection away. But the damned hardness was persistent. It was only when he thought of the Twilight Zone episode that had scared him the most, the one where the poor businessman sees a demon on the wing of a plane, that it began to fade. David leaned back and breathed deeply, Miss Margery's voice once more trying to coax him to sleep.

When he opened his eyes again, Max was looking at him. The boy had a disapproving look on his face, as if David had farted out loud or something. David averted his gaze, and Max grunted and turned back around. All the while,

Miss Margery continued to drone on, and on, and on. When class ended, David quickly leapt from his seat. He was out of the classroom before the bell ever stopped ringing.

The very next day, David changed seats, moving to the back of the room. Two months after that, Max was gone, moving out west with his family. For that, David Higgins was thankful.

The haze of recollection lifts, the demon's slippery tendrils withdrawing from David's mind, and his eyes flutter open. The living room seems darker somehow, more foreboding than ever before. He tries to speak, to plead with the vile thing to stop, but all that leaves his throat is a wet groan.

It's the most sound he's made in almost a full year.

The television on the opposite side of the room fades to black, static hissing and popping on its curved surface. The oil slick that is the demon appears on the wall once more, descending until it becomes a bulge in the faded brown rug that has covered the living room floor for more than a decade. The bulge rushes to the side. It looks as if there's a giant beetle under there, one with menacing pincers that will take off inches of his flesh at a time.

Please stop, David thinks.

The demon isn't listening.

His tormentor disappears beneath the bookcase that rests against the wall to the left. David tries to see where it's gone, but his head is positioned at the wrong angle. He has to strain just to catch a fading glimpse from his periphery. And even then, the thing that draws his attention is the framed picture of him and his wife Linh, taken before Natalie was born, when the demon was nothing but a niggling wraith that haunted him only in dreams. Linh was young then, innocent and pure. She barely spoke any English. It would be two decades before cancer would strip her of that youthful visage and send her to an early grave.

The three shelves of books begin to shimmy and shake, drawing David's eye. He looks on in horror as a single tone is pulled from the rest. It is a dusty book, and that dust slowly slides away like sand in a receding wave. The spine starts to bulge and warp as if breathing. *A Tale of Two Cities* becomes not a title, but an accusation.

Inwardly, David screams.

"You don't like Dickens?" the young man named Percy Stout asked. "Really?"

David shrugged. "Never had any use for him, really," he replied. "Just kinda drones on and on."

Percy grinned sheepishly and reached out, handing him a thick book. "Try this one," he said. "It's my favorite."

"Your favorite, eh?" said David. He looks down at the heavy book in his hand. "Isn't this the one that starts with that best of times, worst of times garbage?"

"The same," Percy said, his smile growing. "It isn't garbage, though. Life isn't all about ramming your shoulder into people while wearing twenty pounds of body armor. Trust me, you'll like it."

"If you say so."

They both turned and walked down the

hall, weaving through the throng of students. Some shouted David's name as he passed them by, others raised their hand for a high-five. A few of the girls lingered shyly by the lockers, fluttering their eyes at him. David beamed as he threw his arm over Percy's shoulder, appreciating the newfound notoriety. He'd finally done it; after three years of trying, he'd at last been promoted to starting linebacker on the football squad. For the first time, he looked forward to seeing his mother's face staring at him with pride instead of the persistent disappointment she always displayed for him. He had a feeling his senior year would be the best of his life.

But still, despite his joy, a large part of him that resided just below the surface cried. David glanced at Percy, at the smooth contours of his jaw and the way his blond hair swept in a wave to the side. There weren't many times that he thought of the moment five years ago when he'd first discovered his hidden feelings for the boy named Max, but ever since meeting Percy over the summer, that had all changed. Percy played sax in the school band, and it was one day after summer football practice that they happened across each other on school grounds. He was a sensitive sort, a head shorter than David and seemingly frail. But he had a great sense of humor and was able to draw people in. From the first moment they spoke, it was like they'd been friends forever. They'd become inseparable.

Again that buzzing feeling invaded David's abdomen. He did his best to fight it down.

"So I'll see you after school?" Percy asked as they neared the staircase.

"After practice. Four o'clock."

"Got it. We can go over my trig notes then. You can drive me home, right?"

"Okay."

"See you soon."

Percy smiled a bit too warmly and dashed up the stairs two at a time. David hung back as other students brushed past him. He felt his neck flush, and deep down he was a flurry of confliction. He suddenly wanted nothing more than to run up those stairs, swing Percy around, and kiss him.

But he knew he couldn't do that.

Those types of feelings were evil.

He turned around and headed to class instead.

It's never enough. No matter how much the demon shows him, no matter how much its visions torment him and make his blood come to boil, it always wants more.

The evil thing lurches out of the bookcase, leaving the book it'd infested resting still like a casket. It floats through the air in a black mist, soaring right in front of David's vision, a cloud of undulating malevolence. The demon seems to hover there for a moment, mocking him, until it picks up speed and careens toward the opposite wall. David almost can't move his eyes fast enough to keep up. The billowing black cloud then becomes a funnel, streaming toward the lamp resting on a small end table on the other side of the room. The conduit of hatred slides over the lampshade.

David's world is pitched into darkness. His body begins to quake.

David couldn't sleep. He'd tossed and turned in bed for hours while a cold sweat broke out on his forehead, drenching his pillow. He had to get up. Had to get moving. The blaring of the television downstairs was maddening. He couldn't help but think maybe he should go home, to his own bed. Maybe that would make a difference.

A soft groan sounded in the blackness of the room. Someone shifted beside him. A soft hand caressed his back.

"David, lie down," said a groggy voice. "You need sleep."

David reached over and clicked on the lamp sitting on the nightstand. He turned slowly, letting his hair fall in front of his face, and gazed at Percy from between the strands. Percy was up on his elbow, his upper body exposed while his lower was covered with the bedsheet. But David knew he was naked under there...just as David was now. His eyes traced the ribs beneath Percy's slender chest, his small pale nipples, the supple curve of his neck. Earlier that night, his lips had been pressed to that neck, had licked circles around those nipples, had planted tiny kisses on those tender ribs. Those and more were acts performed nearly every night for nearly the last three weeks.

David shivered.

"C'mon," said Percy, patting the now-empty spot next to him. "Come back to me."

David let out a deep breath and shook his head. "I can't."

"You want to get up now, then? I'll do it with you. We'll cook eggs or something."

"No. Your grandma's still watching television," David said.

"It doesn't matter. She probably passed out."

David leaned back, allowing his right hand to slip beneath the sheet hiding Percy's lower body. The beautiful, fragile young man sighed.

"Talk to me, Dave," Percy said.

David opened his mouth, then closed it. He didn't want to tell Percy what had really been keeping him awake. He didn't want to break the heart of the one he now realized was the love of his life. But when he glanced over and saw that look of concern on Percy's face, when he saw the way his dainty nose scrunched up, he knew he couldn't stay silent.

"I can't go," he said. "I'm sorry."

Percy collapsed onto his back, staring at the

ceiling. "But you promised. You sounded excited."

"I know," said David. "But listen…I have my future to think about. I have my mom to help take care of. Donald just got drafted, you know. And I'm supposed to be starting college in a couple months." He sighed. "What we talked about…it can wait."

Percy rolled over, placed a kiss on the back of David's hand. "Dave, listen to me. I hate it here. I hate the people, the judgment. We can't be who we are! There's places out there that'll accept people like us. Places we'll be welcomed, even. You can go to school there. I have my inheritance. We can both get jobs and pay our own way. We can be happy. Screw your family. Your mom doesn't really like you, anyway."

"Easy for you to say. Your family's dead." He inclined his head toward the floor, and the television blaring beneath it. "All you got is your grandma, and she's doesn't even remember your name half the time. Why else would we do what we do here and not at my mom's?"

Percy withdrew, looking at him with tears brimming in his eyes. David had never seen anyone look so sad before.

"I'm sorry," he said. "That wasn't called for."

"That's right, it wasn't," said Percy.

David leaned over, putting on his best reassuring voice. "Listen, the time's just not right. We'll go eventually, I promise. We'll build the life we want. I just need time. Please, Percy, give that to me."

Percy looked at him sidelong, concentrating as if each word he spoke deserved to be analyzed like a complex math equation. "You promise?" he asked.

David wanted to tell him he couldn't promise him anything, but he kept his mouth shut. He and Percy had grown so close over their last year of high school. They'd become part of each other's lives. They'd become lovers and partners by every definition of the words. All of it combined to make David doubtful of everything—his wants, his needs, the very nature of his being. Being with a man in this way...all his life, he'd been taught it was a sin. He'd been taught it was evil. And now he was doing it.

If he ran away, his mother would surely find out, and then she'd disown him. No matter *how much their relationship had wavered from sour to grudgingly prideful over the years, the last thing he wanted was to throw away his mother's love. It was Percy who wanted this, it was Percy who was comfortable in his own skin. All David wanted to do was fit in and not make a fuss.*

"I promise I will," David said, drawing forth a smile from the love of his life.

"I'll hold you to that," Percy replied. The lithe man then leaned forward, and their lips met.

While they kissed, and during the moments of passion that came afterward, thoughts of doubt and sin and evil never once crossed David's mind.

Time comes back to him like an unwanted tumor, speeding up and bringing David into the here-and-now. The demon's oil slick lifts off the lamp, once more bathing the living room with light. David's heart beats out of control; his breathing comes in rasping gasps and the machine that controls his lungs has a hard time keeping pace. The device pings and beeps ever more rapidly.

The conversation in the kitchen is still going on, feminine voices cackling with laughter. Natalie doesn't seem to hear the commotion. David thinks that the woman who had come to visit is an agent of the demon that haunts him. It has brought her along to distract his daughter, to allow the haunt to torment him in private.

Please, Natalie...please pay attention, he thinks, but Natalie is nowhere to be found.

The demon, however, is. It takes the form of a wriggling black centipede, circling down the leg of the end table and scurrying across the carpet. It climbs up the leg of the coffee table in the center of the room. There are magazines stacked atop the table, ones that have gone unopened in God knows how long. The centipede stops in the middle of the clutter and rises up on its many legs. The thing faces David, and seems to be laughing.

The demon is mocking him.

A spasm rocks David's left shoulder, and his hand slips off his wheelchair's armrest. His arm dangles there like a dead tree limb, useless, empty, and heavy. David's body is twisted at an odd angle, and the pain is excruciating, even for one who's been wracked with constant pain for years.

The black centipede chatters and falls back down flat. It becomes liquid, seeping into the many dust-covered magazine covers, staining them, darkening them, making them evil. The magazines flutter to life, pages rifling as if caught in a gale-force wind experienced only by the coffee table.

And David is sent back once more.

There wasn't anything interesting to read on the table in the army recruiter's office. Nothing but dog-eared copies of Life *and* Time, *five years old at the earliest, and a stack of wrinkled brochures proclaiming the glory of the Armed Forces. It was as if the implementation of the draft had made the Army stop trying even slightly to impress their potential recruits.*

He'd come home during Thanksgiving break his sophomore year in college to find his mother in tears. Donald, his brother, had died in Vietnam. His mother was inconsolable. Donald had always been her favorite. David reminded her too much of his father, she'd often said, the man who'd left them all high and dry after David was born. And now Donald was gone. "It should've been you!" his mother screamed at him. "It should've been you!"

After that tongue lashing, he'd left the house and spent the night at Percy's. He cried in his arms, railing against the unfairness of it all while Percy's grandma waddled about downstairs, blissfully unaware. The loss of his brother, the loss of his mother's love, the fact he could never make himself reveal their relationship to a single living soul; all of it conspired to break him.

"If it should've been me, then I'll give her that wish," David told Percy.

Oh, how Percy protested. "You can't join the army," he pleaded. "You can't go to Vietnam. I'll be alone without you. You're all I have!" But David was stalwart. This was what he now wanted. No more college, no more sports. He'd get a gun and a uniform, and he'd do everything he could to punish those who'd ripped his brother away from him, who'd made his mother not love him anymore.

That morning he'd left Percy in tears and

stormed straight to the recruiter's office. No second thoughts, no wavering. For the first time in his life, David Higgins was all action.

The front door opened, and David glanced up from watching his jittery knees to see Percy enter the room. He looked delicate as usual, his frame much too slender, his hips much too narrow, but there was something about the expression he wore that chilled David to the bone. Percy walked up to the window, received a clipboard from the receptionist, and then sat down two chairs away from David. He began filling in his forms, eyes intent on the paper.

David leaned over. "Percy, what're you doing?" he whispered.

Percy's eyes flicked toward him, but he never moved his head nor said a word. He kept filling out the form.

"C'mon, Percy, this is stupid. What's going on with you?"

Finally, Percy slipped the pen back under the clipboard's clasp, stood up with a huff, stormed across the waiting room, and placed it on the windowsill. It wasn't until he was back to sitting that he turned in David's direction.

"You want to act rashly?" he said in a quiet

yet stern voice. "Well, so can I."

David instantly got goose bumps. It was completely out of place, but to hear Percy talk in such a way excited him. "You don't understand," he said.

"Doesn't matter what I understand or don't," he said. "All you need to understand is that I'm not gonna be alone again. You go to 'Nam, I go to 'Nam. That's just the way it is."

"But Percy—"

"But nothing, Dave. My mind's made up. Paperwork's all signed." He slapped his hands together as if knocking dirt off them. "What's done is done."

After that they sat in silence, until the recruiter came forward and asked David to come to his office. He cast a final glance into the waiting room before the door was shut and saw Percy sitting there, looking angry and brittle at the same time. He was like a pissed-off china doll, and in his mind's eye David saw that china doll lashing out at a wall in anger and shattering to bits.

He shuddered as the door closed behind him.

Stop it! David strains to tell the beast. *Stop it now!*

But the demon won't stop. Its mass lifts from the magazines in a gelatinous wad of black goop. The pages fall still, covers intact, as if they were never disturbed. The wad of gunk then writhes and becomes a ball that rolls off the coffee table. David strains to see it, watching the rolling ball of hate grow ever closer to him before veering off to the side, where it disappears beneath the fringe of the couch sitting against the far wall. For a long while, all is still.

David's breathing slows down. *All a dream,* he tells himself. *Just a freaking dream.* He spots movement from the corner of his eye and glances over. Natalie is standing in the doorway, a rag held in her hands. Her skin is creamy and bronzed, like her mother's, and her eyes reveal half of her ancestry. When she smiles, it is like the stars realigning after a prolonged era of suffering.

"Dad, everything okay?" she asks.

David wants to reply to her. He wants to tell her about the demon beneath the couch, but no matter how hard he tries to tell his muscles to move, they won't obey him. It is like his body is a prison that he'll never leave.

Natalie walks over to him, kisses him gently on the cheek. She straightens his torso, lifts his arm back into position, and fidgets with the roses in the vase beside him. She checks the machines that control his breathing, making sure they're running properly. David can't see her, can't force his eyes to roll that far in their sockets, and it's like she's not there even though he can hear her fiddling around with knobs and switches.

"Nat, where are you?" calls a voice from the kitchen.

"I'll be right there!" Natalie shouts back. She reappears in David's vision, smiling though there is a hint of sadness in her eyes. "I love you, Dad," she says.

I love you too, sweetie, David thinks. *Please don't leave me.*

It comes out in a bubbling groan.

"I'll be right in the kitchen, okay?" his daughter says. She places another kiss on his head and glides out of the room.

Natalie, no! Natalie, come back!

But she's gone.

There is more movement from the corner of his vision. David aims his eyes in the opposite direction, and if he had the ability to open his mouth and shriek, he would've done so right then and there.

The demon is no longer hiding. It is no longer a formless mass of black gunk. It now holds the shape of a man, a hard man, a strong man, a man who has hatred in his heart and violence in his blood. The broad shoulders move up and down with each breath, and though the form is featureless and black as a stormy night sky, David knows exactly who it is. The thing's head turns in his direction, and David looks deep into the void where its eyes should be. It is like gazing into the abyss, only instead of hellfire, there is nothing.

Absolutely nothing, only blackness.

David stayed as far back from the sergeant as he could while the platoon made their way along a slender path crowded with overgrowth from the surrounding jungle. The sergeant's name was John Pembroke, and he was a huge, burly bastard. While the rest of the enlisted men trudged through these godforsaken jungles grumbling about the desire to be back home, Pembroke took to the sufferable conditions as if there was no place he'd rather be. David himself had seen the grin on the man's face as he plunged his knife into the throat of a young Vietnamese woman suspected of supporting the VC, but he'd done nothing to stop him from killing her. He wasn't alone. None of the other men did either. They were too afraid to.

With each passing day, David tried harder and harder to keep his distance from the man. Pembroke was from Oklahoma, the type of man who would quote scripture one minute and take glee in bringing pain to all around him the next. A headstrong man. Dangerous. Yet that same sort of man was what the Army truly wanted, for there were no better attributes for a wartime soldier than headstrong and dangerous.

"We there yet?" asked the soldier beside him, his tone exhausted beyond belief.

"Shush, Percy," David said out the corner of his mouth.

"I'm just—"

"Hey!" snapped Pembroke from the front of

the line, swiveling around to face his charges. "No talking, only marching!"

Booted feet clomped together. The procession continued.

David glanced over at Percy as they walked. He had thick purple bags under his eyes and his face was slathered with sweat. Angry red welts dotted his formerly flawless skin from where insects had fed on him. He looked frailer than ever, his too-large helmet teetering atop his head, and the rifle draped on his back made him look like a child playing at being a soldier rather than the real thing. Percy looked his way, and David shoved him away harshly. Percy pouted, falling further back in line. David felt instantly guilty, but he didn't want to bring on Pembroke's wrath again, especially after last time.

They'd been in 'Nam for three months now, and each passing day was worse than the last. Every morning brought with it a sense of bone-numbing fear, even though the firefights they'd been engaged in were sparse. The land they moved through was already occupied, after all—though that was sure to change once they entered Quang Tri. That, however, didn't stop the fear of being found by the enemy in the middle of the night and slaughtered.

David feared more for Percy than his own life. Percy wasn't fit for warfare. He was fit for the more refined things in life, not trudging through mile after mile of muck with a rifle held above his head. He was meant to bring joy and light to the world, not death. David wanted nothing more than to wrap him in his arms and make him disappear from this place, rip open a portal through space and time and send Percy back home where he belonged.

Yet despite how much he cared, despite how much he wanted to protect the man he loved, he dared not do anything. His fellow soldiers, Pembroke included, were beginning to grow wary of Percy. They called him faggot and queer and cocksucker, and even though Percy did his best to hide his true nature, acting the brusque man and laughing at the dirty jokes told by his mates, just as David did, he had a certain way about him, a sort of feminine quality that he couldn't veil no matter how hard he tried. The fear they might be discovered caused David to withdraw. He hadn't spoken more than a word to Percy in more than two weeks; well, words that weren't insulting barbs, that is. He would join the others in their taunts and do his best to ignore the look of hurt that came over Percy each time. At night he would lie awake, and he swore he could hear his lover crying in his tent.

I'm sorry, Percy.

At the edge of a river, just as dusk threatened to cast the jungle into blackness, Pembroke called a halt to the march. Tents were set up; canteens were pulled from; disgustingly bland dinners were devoured. There was nervous, lighthearted banter and quiet laughter. The song of the jungle rose in volume as darkness claimed the land, millions of wild things surrounding them on all sides, each and every one of them threatening in their invisibility.

Death lurked in every corner of a land that was nothing but corners.

David slipped into his one-man pup tent and fell into a fitful sleep, only to be awoken by shrieking. He scurried out from under the canvas enclosure, knocking his head against the support rod in the process, nearly toppling his tent. He fumbled for his rifle and rose up. His whole body quaked.

His eyes adjusted to the lack of light, and

David saw that it was nearing dawn. A few streaks of purple daubed the sky. The camp seemed to be empty; only he and six others of the twenty-four soldiers they traveled with emerged from their tents. All looked at one another, eyes wide with fear. The shrieking came again, sounding from somewhere farther along the riverbank. David knew that sound, that voice, just as much as he recognized the spates of cruel laughter that followed.

Without a word and ignoring the confused queries of his mates, David darted along the riverbank in near-darkness, feet churning. Not more than a hundred feet away, he emerged from the foliage into a soggy fjord. The early morning grew all the brighter, and he could plainly see his fellow soldiers there, standing in a circle. In the center of that circle rose Pembroke's head. The man muttered, spittle flying from his lips. His shoulders hunched aggressively, as if he was kicking at something in the center of the circle that the surrounding soldiers blocked. David heard a thud and another scream of pain.

"Hey, Sarge, Higgins is here," one of the men said. David had been so focused on

Pembroke that he hadn't realized he'd been seen.

Pembroke turned in his direction, and the wall of soldiers parted. He stormed across the muddy ground, a wicked-looking grin on his face. David swallowed his fear and stood with feet shoulder length apart, holding his rifle with both hands before him. "What's going on, Sarge?" he asked. It took his every effort to make his voice not sound as sheepish and afraid as he felt.

"We caught him," Pembroke said. A perverted sort of pride oozed out in his tone.

"Caught who, Sarge?"

"The faggot, Higgins. Had Johnston go to him tonight, say he'd been watching him. Said they could find someplace quiet and 'talk.' Ha! Talk!"

Johnston, his face half hidden by shadow, leaned forward. "The queer tried to kiss me," he said disdainfully.

"Probably wanted to suck you off," Pembroke shouted over his shoulder. He then turned back to David, his expression suddenly hard as stone and accusatory. "You knew him before coming here, right? You know he was a faggot all along?"

David tried his best to ignore Percy's whimpers. "Nope," he said. "Never knew."

"Faggots don't belong in the jungle," said Pembroke.

"Sure as fuck don't!" shouted another of the soldiers.

David wanted to puke. He wanted to knock Pembroke out, grab Percy, and run away. But he did none of that. Instead, he said, "They sure don't."

Percy's bawls grew in volume.

"Shut that cocksucker up!" Pembroke roared.

A heavy sound followed, a fist striking a face. David swore he heard a crack. He then stepped forward, past Pembroke and toward the ring of his mates. They stepped aside for him, revealing Percy, laying on his side in the mud, face covered with blood and grime and bruises. David had to hold his breath to keep from passing out.

"Tell me, boys...we're in a land where there's no rules. What do you think should happen to a faggot in a place like this?"

David had no answer for him, but the others sure did.

It wasn't my fault, you did this! David pleads as the shimmering, blackened shape of John Pembroke rises from the couch. The thing takes two lumbering steps forward, and then loses all form. It becomes a tidal wave of oil, falling to the carpet in a splash. It forms a lake of rippling black, like a dead sea in the middle of the living room. That lake soon becomes a river that flows ever toward him.

Stop! Go away! NATALIE!

But there is no help for David Higgins, and he knows it. Hell has come back for him. The demon has arrived to take payment for his sins.

The oily river flows up the stand next to his wheelchair. It is so close now that if he could move at all, he could reach out and sink his fingers into the disgusting slop. But all he can do is look on, his heart hammering out of control, as the demon's essence slithers into the vase beside him, right on the edge of his vision. Almost instantly, the roses in the vase turn black, charred, dead.

David is frightened, more frightened than he's ever been before.

A slimy feeler reaches out for him and turns his head.

His muscles scream at him, his nerve endings fire in agony. He looks at the vase and the demon that lies within, and in the clear, reflective surface of the vase, he sees a reflection. Only it isn't *his* reflection. It is someone else, someone younger, someone with wind-swept blond hair, delicate features, and kind blue eyes. In David's panic, the machine beside him begins beeping out of control.

Not you. No, please, not you.

Percy knelt there in the fjord, but he no longer cried. He must have been beyond tears at that point. All he did was breathe slowly, in and out, and stare at the muddy ground. He never even reacted when his fellow soldiers, men who were supposed to have his back, marched around him in a circle, clouting him upside the head, kicking him in the stomach, violently ripping at his hair.

Even David joined in. His sense of self-preservation made it impossible to do otherwise.

Finally, Pembroke called an end to the games. David merged with the rest of his platoon, standing with hands clasped behind his back at the edge of the river, staring down at his ravaged lover. Percy muttered something beneath his breath, something David couldn't quite hear. He was glad he couldn't.

Pembroke stood before them, shoulders rising and falling as he huffed. For a moment David thought that this would be enough. That Percy's torment was over.

He was right and wrong at the same time.

The sergeant whirled around and stormed up to Percy, ripping his sidearm from his holster in the process. The men of the platoon gasped, but none, including David, moved to stop him. The large man pressed the barrel of the gun to Percy's temple. Percy slowly moved his head, peering up at Pembroke with eyes that now seemed dead. There was no pleading in them, no admonitions, no nothing. He simply stared past Pembroke, as if the man looming above him, holding a gun to his head, wasn't there at all.

"Faggot," Pembroke said.

He pulled the trigger.

One side of Percy's head caved in, the other side exploded. Blood, skull, and brain matter flew, splattering the jungle muck. The body flopped over, rocked in a spasm, and then fell still. The men of the platoon gasped and shouted. One of them even ran up to Percy's corpse, shoving it onto its back, straightening the neck as if he could somehow revive it.

But not David Higgins. David did nothing but turn around and head back to camp as Pembroke shouted orders at the others. There were tears in his eyes, but he wouldn't let them fall. His insides were a raging ball of torment. Percy would never return home; Percy would never again kiss him; Percy would never again offer that smile that could light up a room. Simply thinking of it was nearly enough to drive him insane.

And so David allowed himself to speak, uttering five words under his breath, between his quiet sobs, that would damn him for the rest of his life.

"At least it wasn't me."

David's life flashes before him. He sees the

entirety of his involvement in Vietnam, a war that would end before his platoon ever reached Quang Tri, and his own unspeakable acts. He sees himself in a bar in Laos before heading home for good, sitting solemnly with his mates, their sins unspoken between them. He remembers the sorrow he felt at realizing he would never talk with Percy again; never sit beside a fire in winter wrapped in each other's arms; never again have a person who not only served as a companion, but as a life partner, in each and every way.

He sees the face of the woman he would bring home from that stinking hellhole of a country. He sees the easiness of their relationship, how she wanted nothing but to *get out*, and that at least was something he could give her. He relives their life together in the span of a moment, of Linh sitting at home as he went on business trips—or furtive rendezvous with men under the guise of business trips. He looks on as his daughter is born, as his loveless marriage ends when Linh succumbs to breast cancer.

He sees it all, and his insides begin to burn.

The vase of roses explodes, raining shards of glass down on his unmoving form. Yet Percy's face remains, shimmering in black, staring at him in hatred. Tendrils sprout from his eyes, his mouth, from the gaping wounds in the sides of his head. The face begins to laugh as the tendrils skate toward David, lifting jagged bits of glass, wrapping around his wrist, squeezing like a displeased parent would a naughty child.

"You did nothing," the demon that is Percy grumbles in an inhuman, watery voice. *"You killed me."*

I wanted to help, I did, he says inwardly. *I did all I could.*

"You did nothing when it mattered."

David's mouth falls open. His heart now beats so quickly that it feels like it might explode just as the vase did. His head grows dizzy. He wants to tell Percy that he's sorry, but he can't. For it isn't Percy at all. The demon's features shift, blackness sliding over blackness, until David's own face, washed with darkness and dread, is staring back at him.

The first words that David Higgins

speaks in more than three years is not an apology at all, but the name of the beast before him, the name of his haunt, his damage, his sin, himself.

"*Toi Loi,*" he says, the words nothing but damp a groan. It is all he can muster. He wants to say more, to scream at the top of his lungs, to demand he be forgiven, to announce that what came later washed away his sins. But it would do no good, and as his life slips slowly away, he finally understands the demon's true reason for being.

One evil act cannot make up for another. *Toi loi.*

❦

At least it wasn't me.

It was a proclamation and a curse, an evil thing to think and beyond evil to utter aloud. It had haunted David as he sat in his tent, knees clutched to his chest while Pembroke ordered his charges to dump Percy's body in the muddy river. It haunted him as he dismantled his tent and packed it away in his rucksack. And it haunted him as the platoon continued its march through the ever-oppressive jungle, following the river northeast. A strange, somber aura worked its way through each man present. Every snap of a branch was an accusation; every rustle of leaves in the thick foliage was a monster waiting to devour each of them whole.

And David knew right then that he deserved it. They all did.

As he walked, he saw Percy's face the moment he died. He saw his head snap to the side, saw blood and bone soar through the air. He saw his delicate, beautiful features bruised and bloodied and hopeless.

And yet you did nothing, *a part of him said in accusation.*

There was nothing I could do, *the survivor in him replied.*

You taunted him. You were no better than the others. You're a monster.

David did all he could to silence the voice. Guilt threatened to overwhelm him. In desperation he flipped his culpability over in his mind, twisted it, made it blackened and rotting, just like Percy was now. The guilt turned to anger, bubbling within him until he felt like a ball of rage. His breathing came in quick bursts, his jaw quavered. Suddenly he didn't feel so warm. Suddenly, his every muscle hummed with energy as he took step after step through the swampy wasteland, keeping his eyes ever forward, on the back of Pembroke's head, lest his anger start to fade.

It was nearly dark again, the jungle coming to life all around them, when Pembroke called the order to make camp. The soldiers performed their duties somberly. No one spoke, no one laughed. They all knew what had happened was wrong. They all knew they were partly responsible.

It began raining just as the jungle was swallowed in near-complete darkness. David sat in his tent, jittery, knees pulled up to his chest, while the rest of the camp slept. There was no way he could sleep, not now, maybe not ever again. Percy's death played on a loop behind his eyelids each time he tried. He tilted his head, hearing snores rise above even the sound of the rain. David unhooked his hands from around his knees and slipped out of his tent, tucking his knife into his belt.

It was raining so hard that he could barely see a foot in front of him. His uniform was sodden and heavy. David slipped between the tents, seeking out the largest one, where Pembroke slumbered. When he reached the tent he paused, gathered his breath. His nerve endings were on fire, his vision bathed in red. Finally he ducked down, shoved aside the tent flap, and entered.

He could see nothing inside the squat enclosure, but he could sense Pembroke in there, lying on his side and snoring not three feet away. David grabbed a soggy pack of matches from his pocket and inched closer to the sleeping man. When he could feel Pembroke's breath on his knees, he struck a match. It guttered to life, casting faint, eerie light throughout the tent.

Pembroke's eyes snapped open.

Before the larger man could react, David tossed aside the match, ripped the knife from his belt, and drove it deep into his right eye socket. Again, and again, and again.

In the darkness, warm fluid poured over his hands. David gritted his teeth and brought the knife down one last time, into Pembroke's heart. "I hope it hurts," he whispered. "I hope it fucking hurts." Tears streamed down his cheeks.

David's anger and sorrow slowly waned, replaced by an emptiness that would follow him for the rest of his life. He rose to his feet and grabbed Pembroke's corpse by the legs. He hauled the body out into the rain, trudged past his fellow soldiers' tents, silent in the deluge, and approached the river's edge. He stood there, alone except for his dark thoughts. He leaned over Pembroke's gnarled face. "For Percy," he said.

He shoved the body down the riverbank. The splash it made when it hit water was drowned out by the pouring rain. The rain that would wash away the blood in the same way the downpour and thunder had washed out the sounds of his crime. None would know what he'd done. None could point a finger. It could have been any one of them. The whole platoon had stood there and watched Percy die. No one had spoken up, no one had intervened. They all knew they were partly responsible for Percy's death, and they all knew that any one of them could've been next. They all had motive...

David stood there by the river's edge, watching the corpse roll over as it slowly floated away.

"Toi loi," he said under his breath. Fittingly, it was the only Vietnamese he knew.

Toi loi.
Guilty as sin.

Robert J. Duperre is an author of horror and epic fantasy, as well as a part-time contributor to *Shock Totem* magazine. He has written the post-apocalyptic series *The Rift*, as well as the stand-alone science fiction/fantasy mashup *Silas*. Robert has also edited the short story collections *The Gate: 13 Dark and Odd Tales* and *The Gate 2: 13 Tales of Isolation and Despair*. His latest novel, *Dawn of Swords*, the first book in the new three-book series, *The Breaking World*, written in collaboration with David Dalglish, was just released by **47North**. Robert lives in northern Connecticut with his wife, the artist Jessica Torrant, his three children, and Leonardo, the one-eyed wonder dog.

HOLIDAY RECOLLECTION
HANGING UP THE GLOVES
by John Dixon

My first love was boxing. Every girl played second fiddle to the sport through my teens and early twenties—until I met my wife. Things with her were different—and I mean instantly—and six months into the relationship, when I was poised to go pro, I abruptly hung up the gloves.

I quit on a Tuesday night, after demolishing a kid from Jersey over three ridiculously bloody rounds. That night, my friend, who happens to be a paramedic, pointed out that Tommy Morrison had just contracted AIDS. Think about the guys in the gym, he told me, think about HIV and hep. And for the first time, I did start considering those dangers... and in the back of my mind was Christina, the life I could see us having together, the life, in fact, we were already building. That was it. I never competed again.

It's funny how love can put past infatuation into perspective. Just as some guys say about past girlfriends, "I'll always love her," I will always love boxing...but it wasn't until months later, perhaps around the time that I asked Christina to marry me, that I really had the distance to understand how disastrous a professional boxing career would have been to me. Now, almost twenty years on, I'm thankful every day that I settled on the correct love.

GOLDEN YEARS

by John Boden

"Good Morning, babe," Larry said, leaning to give Mary a peck on her cheek. Her skin tasted like the soap she used, and he hated it. He wished he could gouge out her eye with his grapefruit spoon. He smiled.

"Morning, Love," she replied, sipping her coffee and envisioning the butter knife separating his head from his shoulders. The small silence between them filled with the *scritch-scritch* of the knife spreading butter on her toast.

Larry picked up the paper and started on the local news section. He reached under the newsprint and grabbed a slice of toast from the tray. Clutching the knife, Mary watched as he raised the toast to his mouth, and she wished she had the nerve to sever fingers from hand.

"What time must you go in today, Love?" she asked, licking her thumb and using it to pick up crumbs from her tablecloth. She looked at the paper wall he sat behind and thought about smashing it with the meat cleaver.

"I ought to be there by nine or so, but I'm the boss, so...whenever." He chuckled at the quip—and at the image he held of strangling Mary with the telephone cord. He folded the paper and laid it beside his empty plate. "Better get a move on." He stood and leaned forward to give his wife another little kiss on her cheek. He thought about how simple it would be to turn slightly and bite off her nose. Chew it and swallow it. He smiled and whispered in her ear: "I love you."

Mary stood in the doorway to the bedroom and watched as Larry pulled his work pants on; they were to his knees and he was bent over, pulling them higher.

Hefting the iron skillet in her hand, Mary raised it and stepped forward...

"I love you more," she said.

John Boden lives in the shadow of Three Mile Island, where he bakes cakes and cookies for a living. Any remaining time is unevenly divided between his amazing wife and sons, working for Shock Totem, and a little of his own writing. His unique fiction has appeared in *52 Stitches*, *Metazen*, *Weirdyear*, *Black Ink Horror 7*, *Shock Totem*, and *Psychos*, edited by John Skipp. His not-for-children children's book, *Dominoes*, was published late last year. He has stunning muttonchops.

SCAN

SP

0:00:51   USED

HOLIDAY RECOLLECTION

AKAI

by Jassen Bailey

I'm going to tell you about my very first love. She was a true beauty. Dependable and boy...was she smooth. By today's standards, some would categorize her as full figured and elderly. I loved her just the way she was. Being a youth, I had never seen anything like her. Her name was Akai.

Akai was the first VCR my parents ever purchased. It was the mid-eighties and this was such an exciting purchase. She was a massive gray box that had a plug in remote control. At this point TVs did not have remotes, so this was also my introduction to remotes. She sat on top of our floor model television set, which was encased in a finished wood cabinet. I sat inches from the screen to make it easier to stop/pause the VCR and adjust volume. The cord on the remote was ridiculously short. My sweet Akai lasted for over a decade. She was such a beauty, she introduced me to a whole new world, opening my eyes to the glories of VHS movies and video stores.

As a child, I remember my mom taking me to see *Friday the 13th Part III 3D* in the movie theatre, and to the drive-in to see Jaws. Those were such great times, but to have the ability to see favorite movies whenever you wanted to watch them? Now that was something special.

Video rental shops started popping up all over the town. I was mesmerized by all the horror posters and video covers displayed in the stores. Horror had its own section in each of these establishments. I became obsessed with all the various films and video covers. Movies such as *I Spit on Your Grave*, *Basket Case*, *Sleepaway Camp*, and *Rabid* cooed me in. I coaxed my mom to rent them all for me. And Akai never let me down...

There were weekends I would take in up to seven horror films. I had never known so many existed. My only other exposure to horror films had been on HBO and in the movie theaters. Akai introduced me to Cronenberg, Romero, Gordon, Fulci, and Hooper to name just a few. I started spending more time with her than I did with the boys around the block.

On one particular weekend, I rode my bike to the closest video store with a friend to rent some horror films. Looking forward to spending some serious time with Akai, I ended up stealing the *Texas Chainsaw Massacre Part 2* and *Slumber Party Massacre* box covers. My obsession with these covers led me to fantasize about having the covers displayed around my room at home. My mom (who knew I took the covers) told me when she returned the rentals that the owner had inquired if she knew who could have possibly done this. (I suspect the owner knew as well.) She offered a reward of seven movie rentals to the person who returned the box covers. It didn't take me long to collect the reward. And yes, she gave me the seven free rentals.

My relationship with Akai lasted several years. Though she was eventually replaced in my house with more modern video viewing equipment, she was never replaced in my memory and heart as my first true love.

SHE CRIES

by K. Allen Wood

Under the soft amber glow of the descending moon, the cracked ground stretched away into darkness like crooked timber, and it beckoned David Hardwick to follow.

Setting down his fishing pole and backpack, David stepped out beyond what once had been the edge of Larme Pond, a spring-fed body of water situated north of Lake Quinisonnett. He tested the dry ground with his boot, scuffed it, dug his heel into it, thrust his weight downward. To his amazement, the earth was solid and dusty, as if it had been long deprived of water.

Many things had come and gone from David's life: family, friends, lovers. Jobs and cars and hobbies, and countless other things. Such is life, one might say, and David would agree. Barring major droughts, dams, and aliens invading Earth for its precious resources, ponds and other large bodies of water generally were permanent fixtures a man could rely on being present—and in the same place—his entire life.

For most of his thirty-eight years, ever since his old man had first brought him to this place, Larme Pond had been a constant presence in David's life. He had been out here just last week. Then, the water had been high for this time of year.

But now...

Fascinated, heart racing, David took a tentative step forward.

⁂

Cradled in her arms, Anna Triste watched her son sleep, his tiny chest rising and falling in smooth cadence, much like the silky waves that lapped against her toes.

Above, the sky was almost blurry for so many stars. A warm summer breeze tousled her hair, tickling her neck. She giggled.

Thomas, her husband, her love, lit a cigarette and inhaled. She turned toward him, and nuzzled up closer to his warm body.

"I love you," said Thomas, putting his arm around her and kissing the top of her head. "I'll never leave you again."

Anna closed her eyes and smiled...

When she opened her eyes again, the dream faded to four cold, heartless walls—her prison. A single candle burned low on the table before her. Its meager light revealed the nightmare that sleep, somehow, always kept at bay: Thomas was gone, and she was alone.

How long had it been now? Thomas had left in spring, said he'd return at the turn of winter, but it felt as if centuries had passed. God, she missed him. Tears bloomed, but she blinked them away. Like the painful memories that shadowed her every move and filled her dreams, the tears were always right there at the edge of her vision, an unwanted, threatening presence.

But she was done crying. She had shed too many tears already.

Beside her, the child slept in his cradle. Sometimes, when she looked upon her son, this small reflection of her beloved Thomas, it was as if all were perfect in the world. But when she looked away, she knew her son could never fill the aching hole Thomas had left behind. The babe was a mockery of her misery, his cries silent, his stare accusing. Or maybe he screamed out for her but she was simply too tired to hear his cries.

Or maybe she didn't care. This had often occurred to her, tormented her.

Tonight, though, all Anna cared about was Thomas. Tonight was different. Thomas would come home, finally. She felt it in the air, sensed him drawing nearer to her. She *knew*. He loved her, and she would be here waiting.

She licked her dry lips. She was thirsty, and hungry. Her body ached. But she couldn't leave. If Thomas were to come back while she was away, she would never be able to forgive herself. What if he found the cabin empty and thought she had left him? She could leave a note, but she had nothing with which to write, and Thomas had never been good with reading, anyway. No. She had to stay, had to wait.

And so she remained, holding on to a fine thread of hope, while a small, insistent voice in her mind demanded of her the unthinkable. *Stand!* it seemed to say. *Leave this place, for Thomas has left you, never to return.* The voice echoed through her mind, escalating into a many-mouthed scream.

Anna covered her ears and screamed with it.

Slowly descending toward the middle of the pond, David determined a sinkhole was the only explanation. Mother Earth must have opened up and took a big gulp. He warily continued forward with that in mind, knowing full well that a sinkhole would swallow him as easily as water. A little meat for Mother's drink.

His thinking changed when he came upon a pool of water at the pond's center, maybe fifty feet across. Its surface roiled as if boiling. He saw, however, that it was teeming with life, as if every fish in the lake were here, stuffed into this small pool. Turtles and frogs and crayfish flopped among the aquatic throng.

"Fuck," he said, unable to come up with anything more fitting for the moment. He repeated it a few more times.

David caught himself glancing toward

the sky, looking for those aliens that had invaded Earth for its water. Thankfully, the sky revealed no alien presence, only stars and the moon, which was now a mere sliver above the trees.

On his knees, at the edge of the pool, he tried with his bare hands to catch a trout—some of which were bigger than any he'd ever caught. He laughed like a child as he missed fish after fish, their slimy skin proving too slippery for his grasp. He wished his father were here to witness this phenomenon; he would have gotten a kick out of it, and maybe he'd have had an answer for it all.

As he knelt there in awe, a sound broke across the sloshing water, echoing between the trees along the shoreline.

Standing, David wiped his wet hands on his shirt and brushed dirt from his knees. He looked around, listened. The sound did not come again.

He cautiously moved off in the direction from which he thought the noise had come, a noise which he was now almost certain had been a scream.

Her screams echoed through the tiny room, bouncing from wall to wall, taunting the waiting silence.

When the screams—and the memory of them—faded, Anna reached down and picked up her son, his limbs and head dangling limp as if his bones had turned to dust. She ran her fingers through his soft hair. "I'm sorry for not being strong," she said. "Daddy will be home soon, and everything will be perfect again. Worry not, my dear boy."

Anna unbuttoned her nightgown, let it fall to her waist, and guided her son's mouth to her withered nipple.

David climbed out of the dry and dusty carcass of Larme Pond. The northern shoreline bordered hundreds of acres of thick, overgrown state forest. He'd explored these woods countless times as a child, looking for leprechauns, digging for buried treasure, playing Manhunt with his friends. Here, it was as if only infinite wonder existed, and it offered a child plenty of inspiration to conjure the fantastical.

He continued to listen, but heard nothing save for the faint rustling of insects and small animals in the underbrush. The soft carpet of grass and pine needles hushed his footfalls as he moved forward through the trees. In the distance he saw a faint yellow glow shimmering in the darkness like a ghost. A camp fire perhaps; he couldn't tell. He approached slowly, and as he got closer saw that it was light coming from a single window on the side of a small log cabin.

"What the hell?" he whispered, fully convinced that talking to oneself was a sure sign of sudden onset schizophrenia. And coming upon a cabin in woods where previously there never had been a cabin before did little to dissuade that sort of thinking.

He wondered if he were losing his mind, for in all his years he'd never seen the cabin that clearly stood before him. Lichen and weeds and small saplings filled every crevice, the roof was spotted with large islands of dark green moss. The smell of damp rot permeated the air around the cabin, indicating to David that it had been there for a long time.

Which defied logic.

Dreaming, he thought. *You, sir, are obviously dreaming.* But wasn't the dreamer supposed to be oblivious to the dream?

He sidled up to the dirty window and peered inside.

If the cabin appeared small from the outside, the space within was tiny. Inside, to the right of the window, stood something out of time: a cradle made from a hollowed-out log. It rested on a wooden frame, which itself was adorned with an intricate carving of the sun. A thing made out of love, and a sharp contrast to the dirty, unkempt blanket and small pillow that lay inside it. A lumpy stained mattress sat in the corner next to the cradle, its blankets and pillows in equal disarray and squalor.

Crouched in the corners of the room, shadows swayed hypnotically as the flame from a single candle danced in the middle of a rough-hewn wooden table. A woman sat staring into the candle's flame as it burned low. Pressed to her left breast was a small child; her right breast lay bare.

Shocked and embarrassed, David ducked below the windowsill so fast, his lower jaw slammed against its edge. His teeth sunk into the flesh of his tongue.

He cried out.

From inside the cabin, he heard the unmistakable sound of chair legs scraping on a wooden floor.

"Fuck," he said again. *Mind your tongue, Davey*, he could hear his mother admonish. *Cussing is the language of the inarticulate.*

Backing away into the cover of a thick copse of shrubs and saplings, David crouched down into the shadows.

The cabin door opened, and the woman, still holding the baby to her now-covered chest, looked out into the dark. "Thomas," she said. "Is that you?"

When no answer came, the woman stepped out onto the rickety landing. She scanned the darkness and stopped her gaze at the exact spot where David crouched. He sucked in his breath and swallowed the air as if he were about to freedive to the bottom of the Great Blue Hole. He could taste the salty thickness of his own blood as it seeped from his wounded tongue and trickled down his throat.

"Thomas?" the woman asked again.

Not wanting to alarm her by running, making her think he'd been up to no good, David came out of his crouch and stepped forward. He waved shyly. "I—" he started, then paused. The woman was smiling, and though it showed no indication of malice, he shivered. "I'm...I...ma'am, I'm sorry. My name's David. I was out fishing and, or trying to, anyway, and—"

"I'm Anna," she said. "Do you have any water, perhaps something to eat, some cheese or bread?"

"Any...?" David shook his head, confused. "No, I'm sorry. I don't."

Even under the delicate light of the coming dawn, David could see disappointment cross her face like storm clouds marring a summer sky.

"Perchance, are you an acquaintance of Thomas's?" she asked. "Will he be returning soon?"

"Not sure, ma'am. I'm afraid I don't

know anyone named Thomas. I was just—"

She cocked her head slightly, as if she were just then seeing him for the first time. "Do you travel from the west? Do you know of the mill workers?"

"No," he said. "I live a few miles from here, not far."

"A curious man, you are." She was silent for a moment, head bowed, then looked up and said, "Do you have any water?"

Again he told her no, and again her smile dipped, her eyes downcast in apparent sadness. "Perhaps from the pond," she said. "If it be no trouble to you."

David was about to tell her the pond was dry, but he thought of the deep pool at its center. "I suppose I could get you some," he said. A smile widened across Anna's haggard face. "But I'm not sure it's safe to—"

"Come in," she said. "I'll find you a pail."

David hesitated, but when it became clear that Anna was waiting for him to follow, he quickened his pace. What harm could come from such a frail thing?

He followed her through a small foyer, and then into the cabin's single room. It appeared even smaller and darker from the inside. A tattered copy of Dickens's *The Cricket on the Hearth* lay open on the table. David thumbed through its pages. Like everything else, it looked and felt real, but also out of time, as if it didn't quite belong in *this* moment.

Then again, he was slowly beginning to feel like it was he who didn't belong.

The air was musty and oppressive, seemingly weighted down with despair. *Dead air*, he thought. Something David knew all too well...

Before his mother passed, she had clung to this world for six long months, valiantly fighting the cancer which they all knew would eventually destroy her. Day after day, David and his father had witnessed the relentless, destructive force of the disease as it feasted. Her skin turned a sickly gray-green, she choked on her teeth as they fell from her rotting gums. Death crawled through her, over her, molesting and befouling her before their eyes. It had filled his childhood home with its vile presence, its evil promise of total annihilation. They were helpless. And now it was here, in this very room.

The raw stench of Death.

Anna went to the cradle and dropped the baby into it as if it were a ragdoll. The baby didn't cry out, but David could see the way its head was cocked that it should have.

"Maybe I should go," he said, taking a step backward.

Anna didn't seem to hear. On tiptoe, she rummaged through a deep-set cubbyhole in the cabin's back wall. Her short nightgown had risen above her hips, revealing to David that she wore nothing beneath. He could see pubic hair and the lips of her vagina jutting down between her skeletal legs, which were themselves covered in bruises and scars, her waist all sharp angles of bone.

"Here it is," she said. David quickly looked away as she turned around, his cheeks burning. She held out a rusty bucket reverently, as though it were an offering to a god.

David stepped forward, grasped the handle, and took the bucket from her shaking hands. She was still smiling.

"Please," she said, "I'm so thirsty. I can't

leave. Thomas is due home from the mill, and my baby—" She stopped, gestured toward the cradle.

"Ma'am, is everything okay here?" David asked. "I mean—I could get help, if you need it."

Anna looked down at her feet and fidgeted with the lacing around the neck of her nightgown. "Fine, everything's fine," she replied. "Thomas will be home soon, and everything will be fine."

David knew that was bullshit. This cabin, this woman, her unmoving baby—his entire morning, for that matter—was anything but fine.

"I'll get the water," he said, holding up the bucket, its handle rattling and echoing through the bare room. "Be right back."

"Thank you. Bless your heart, David." She grabbed him by the arm, startling him, and kissed his cheek. Her breath assaulted his senses like the stink from a long-dead animal, but he blushed all the same.

She followed him out onto the landing, thanking him again and again, her happiness visibly splayed across her tired, sickly face.

But David had lied to her. He had no intention of ever going back to the cabin in the woods. He was going home, to call the sheriff.

Probably to report a murder.

Anna watched David disappear into the woods, while the world around her slowly came alive with the coming sun.

She cried.

Though she had promised herself that she was done with crying, she cried. And it felt good. *Wonderful.* She had found a reason to hope, to truly have faith again.

David would help her, if only until Thomas returned. She was saved.

And so she cried.

The rusty bucket rattled in David's hand as he stomped his way across the pond bottom. His shoes left imprints of his passing in the soft earth.

Sympathy and uncertainty tugged at his

heartstrings, and he found himself heading toward the pool at the center of the pond. He was torn. Should he get the water, bring it back to the strange woman in the cabin, and then go home and call for help? If one thing was clear, she needed help. Or should he just go straight home, make the call to the sheriff?

The clattering bucket tormented his indecisiveness.

He stopped and cursed himself for ever having looked through that window. He knew this area, knew that cabin did not belong and should not be there. But then, how many years had passed since he'd last been in the woods on the other side of the pond? Twenty years, at least. Not since childhood. Could someone have been living out there like a frontierswoman for that long? He supposed it was possible.

Though Anna's words gnawed at him. *Do you know of the mill workers? Thomas is due home from the mill.* There hadn't been any active mills in the area for at least fifty years.

Frustrated, David raised his arm, fully intent on hurling the bucket—and with it his promise to Anna—into the brightening morning. But his hand was empty, the bucket gone. He looked around, but saw nothing of the old metal thing. *Must have dropped it*, he thought. Dropped it while pondering the strange business of Anna and her dead baby.

Without the bucket, though, his decision was made. David stalked off toward the fishing gear he'd left on the opposite shore.

The morning brightened further, birdsong filled the warming air. As he trudged along, David gradually felt the change beneath his feet. Only when his right foot slipped out from underneath him and he crashed to the ground—now a soggy, muddy mess—did he realize just how much it had changed.

He'd been too busy chasing the dizzying thoughts spinning around his head, trying to sort through everything that had happened. He half-expected to wake up at any moment, in his own bed, as the fuzzy tendrils of this bizarre dream receded into nothingness. But the cool water that seeped through his jeans felt too real, too cold to be a dream.

He slowly stood, centering his balance. The sun had not yet fully broken the tree line, but as the day continued to engulf the night David could see the reflective glimmer of light upon water.

In all directions.

Again he found himself fascinated. The pond was filling with water, it bubbled up through the ground all around him. He shifted his feet, and in the slick clay mud he nearly toppled over again.

Time to go.

As he hurried along, the mud became more treacherous. The ground clutched at his feet so greedily that he kept looking down expecting to see the bony hands of the dead wrapped around his ankles. He was reminded of the pool scene in *Poltergeist*, and he quickened his pace. Water sloshed as he pushed forward, but the faster he went the slower he seemed to move. His panic rose with the water. When his left leg sank deep into the sucking mud, up to his knee, fear churned up his insides.

David pulled at his stuck leg, but the harder he pulled the deeper his other leg sank. Before long, both legs were entrenched deep in the mud. He yanked and twisted and thrashed about.

The water deepened.

Frantic, David screamed for help. He watched the water rise past his waist and steadily up his chest. He cried out to his father, to God, and even to Anna. He prayed that someone—*anyone*—would hear.

The water reached his quivering chin. David lunged below the surface and tried to dig his legs out of the mud. He managed to loosen—but not free—his right leg.

He came up for air. His head broke the surface, but his mouth was now under water. He titled his head back and inhaled deeply through his nose.

The sky above was a dim blue, spotted with bruise-purple clouds. Birds soared across the sky, free as air.

Free as air...

Inhaling again, David disappeared into the water. He tore at the mud, handful after handful, until his right leg came loose.

Head pounding, chest feeling as if it were about to explode, he continued to dig.

Somehow, his left leg sunk deeper, but he managed to liberate it enough to hope.

His lungs demanded to be fed.

David straightened his body and stretched his neck, anticipating that cool touch of oxygen.

It never came.

Cold realization struck him as if a mountain had crumbled atop his helpless body. David thrust himself toward the surface and the air he knew was just millimeters away, flapping his arms with all the strength he could muster.

He never moved.

He reached up and absurdly tried to pull the water *down*.

Terror crushed his resolve. His mouth opened wide...and he inhaled. The water rushed into him unhindered. It tasted salty, like cold, bitter tears. Pain exploded within his chest as if he were being eaten by the lust of a thousand sorrows.

He continued to struggle for the surface. And then, almost in an instant, the pain receded; a calm fell over him, a serene assurance that there was nothing left to fear. A tranquility he'd never known before.

Peace, he thought. And it was beautiful.

His vision blurred, and his body tingled as a small seed of regret blossomed in his gut. He thought of his father, his friends, even Anna, felt as if he'd failed them all.

A deep chill settled over him. His body shuddered. David Hardwick opened his mouth to cry out...

Anna lay in bed. Fresh tears welled in the corners of her eyes and streamed down her temples, onto her pillow. Outside, birds chattered and sang their songs, their jubilant music flittering through the morning.

Just before dawn broke across the water, the candle illuminating the inside of the cabin went out. A lazy curl of smoke snaked its way toward the ceiling.

Anna watched it, thought of David, her savior, and smiled. She thought Thomas, of welcoming him home, then pulled the blankets tighter around her, closed her eyes, and dreamed.

K. Allen Wood's fiction has appeared in *52 Stitches, Vol. 2*; *The Zombie Feed, Vol. 1*; *Epitaphs: The Journal of New England Horror Writers*; *The Gate 2: 13 Tales of Isolation and Despair*; *Anthology Year One*; *Appalachian Undead* and its companion chapbook, *Mountain Dead*; and most recently in *Anthology Year Two: Inner Demons Out*. He lives and plots in Massachusetts.

For more info, visit his website at www. kallenwood.com.

Holiday Recollection

THE SAME DEEP WATER AS YOU

by Bracken MacLeod

In my early twenties, I didn't know that you can't save people from themselves and ended up learning that lesson over and over again. Youth is the teacher of fools.

In '91 I was smitten with a woman named Jill, who was soulfully intellectual and beautiful. However, she was also deeply, clinically depressed over a recently failed marriage and the pressures of grad school and being a single mother. I arrogantly convinced myself I could be the rock she and her son clung to for support in bad weather and that eventually together we'd walk out of the sea into bright sunlight and lie down in tall, soft grass. She never got the professional help she needed and ended up violently killing herself. The storm that followed tore at my heart and mind and propelled me through two more increasingly destructive relationships that alienated my friends and drove me deeper into despair.

That lasted until I met the actual love of my life. But even after I married her, it took the better part of a decade for me to stop blaming myself for being unable to save Jill. She still haunts me on occasion. That was the worst.

Holiday Recollection
ONE LUCKY HORROR NERD

by James Newman

"Share with me your morbid love, we are the living dead." —from "Tonight (We'll Make Love Until We Die)," by SSQ, on the *Return of the Living Dead* soundtrack

"See how she sets you on fire...black candy is so hard to find." —from "Black Candy," by Danzig

I am a lucky man in so many ways. I'm married to a woman who is a shining example of a perfect wife and mother. That's the most important thing, of course. But as it relates to this fine publication, I'd like to talk for a few minutes about how fortunate I am to have bagged myself a "horror chick."

My wife, Glenda, puts up with a lot. My obsession with monsters, madmen, and everything in between is just one of the many things she tolerates about me. There's an ongoing joke we share between us that pretty much says it all: Glenda tells me, "You can remember the name of the guy who used to be the hairdresser for the woman who was married to the director of that cheesy killer clown flick from 1979, but it always slips your mind when I ask you to take out the trash?"

And I have no retort. She has a point, and it pierced my heart a long time ago.

The only thing my woman ever complains about, in fact? It's not the twenty to thirty hours a week I stay logged on to Netflix, constantly looking for a new horror film to impress me or just revisiting forgotten faves from years ago; it's not the hundreds (thousands?) of dollars I spend annually on books by my favorite writers of dark fiction. It's not the way I "check out" of the real world while I'm hard at work on my latest writing project. The only thing that ever seems to bother her about my infatuation with the horror genre is...well, I'll just let her say it: "You don't write enough."

I got a good one, didn't I? No doubt about it. And did I mention she can be my toughest critic when it comes to my own work? Yep...

Glenda doesn't tell me what I want to hear, she tells me what I *need to know*. Such honesty is invaluable to any writer who wants to continually improve at his or her craft.

The cool thing is, she digs this stuff, too. How could I *not* fall head-over-heels in love with a woman who cites *The Exorcist III: Legion* as her "favorite scary movie," a woman who prefers watching episodes of *Dexter*, *Bates Motel*, and *American Horror Story* to *Keeping Up with the Kardashians*?

Every few years, we throw a massive Halloween bash, and Glenda gets into the extensive decorating and dressing up just as much as I do (one year we were Frankenstein and the Bride, another a sated vampire and his victim in her blood-soaked nightgown, then the next year we switched it around so Glenda was the bloodsucker and I was the pajama-clad victim with his necklace of garlic and crosses that hadn't done a damn bit of good). We love to read together, too. I know that's incredibly nerdy, but I couldn't care less. We've been together for a little over twenty-two years as I write this, and for at least twenty of those years we've enjoyed sharing good books. How does that work, you ask? Well, usually it entails reading aloud to her as she soaks in the bathtub or cooks dinner for our family. Traditionally, we read every new Joe Lansdale and Bentley Little title together, not long after they're published (we're currently about halfway into the latter's *The Influence*, by the way, and it's fantastic), although we've enjoyed plenty of other great writers together as well.

Through the years, Glenda has accompanied me to the occasional horror convention, and these days we take our sons with us to enjoy the freakish festivities (we have a toddler and a teenager...and you think *you* know horror?). They get a kick out of it. Jacob, the little guy, is obsessed with zombies and werewolves, while Jamie's favorite films are *Night of the Creeps* and David Cronenberg's version of *The Fly*. I couldn't be more proud!

Glenda is very much her own person, of course. Opposites attract, as they say. And we're the perfect example of that old cliché. She likes her chick flicks, her Lifetime television, and her Oprah Book Club selections. She doesn't wear horror shirts all the time like I do (although she does have one she wears to the conventions—"YOU CAN'T SCARE ME I'M A NURSE," it boasts—and she'll occasionally wear one of my tamer ones, which I always find incredibly sexy). She doesn't want to see *every* horror film I want to see—she doesn't care for the really gory stuff, but then I'm no huge fan of that, either, without a good story to go along with it. I'm sure I've dragged her to the theater more times than she can count to see some movie that she didn't *really* have much of a desire to see. But she did it for me. And that, my friends, is love.

I suppose I'm getting soft in my old age, 'cause this Valentine's Day I plan to return the favor. This isn't unheard of, but I have to admit it's not something I do very often. Our plans for the evening: A nice steak dinner, followed by a movie she's been looking forward to. It's something called *Labor Day*, and it stars Josh Brolin (*Hollow Man*, *Nightwatch*, *Oldboy*) and Kate Winslet (sorry, but I'm struggling to think of a single genre film she's been in; Glenda would undoubtedly nudge me in the side right now and say, "Go ahead, tell 'em you loved *Titanic*," at which point I would shush her, nervously looking around to make sure no one heard).

Not sure if I mentioned the fact that this *Labor Day* is one of those aforementioned "chick flicks." It might or might not be based on a Nicholas Sparks book.

Yeah.

The scariest thing of all, though?

You wouldn't believe me if I told you. But I will anyway...

I'm looking forward to it.

☉MEN

by Amanda C. Davis

Back when I sold insurance, laying up money to get engaged, I used to tell people, "Death never calls to let you know it's stopping by." If I was feeling jocular, or if they looked like they could appreciate a little gallows humor, I'd go on. Little routine of mine. "You think you see it winking at you sometimes, but death's an awful flirt. Come down with cancer and die of a stroke. Catch bronchitis and go down in a plane crash. Why, I insured a fellow who liked to go hunting. His hunting partner had bad aim and a neverending thirst, if you catch my drift. This fellow had a policy—two million dollars to his widow in case his hunting partner got boozy and decided this guy resembled a ten-point buck. So one day the two of them are hunting, and my fellow tracks a wounded deer through the brush—and right off a cliff."

They usually asked then if the widow got the two million, and I explained it was a special policy, but she got a million under the standard accident coverage—which most people allow isn't bad.

What I'm saying is no death's your own until it's your own, just like no lady's your wife until you marry her. Me, I figured I'd go to the morgue with a toe tag reading "HEART ATTACK." That's what got my father, his father, and half a family plot full of uncles. Heart attack. And then one day I'm walking with my girl and up screams a nutjob in a big car, and—bam! Toe tag. I never even had a chance to propose.

Now, running an omen isn't so different from working an actuarial table—we can't any of us see the future, dead or alive—so I naturally fell into the business after my, ahem, departure. For a while I did a breeze on the same corner where my cold head first hit the pavement. Just whistle gently, tousle a newspaper once in a while. Quiet gig. Got my feet wet.

They moved me to the aviary division before long. Busier. Friendly, though. I had a lot of company in the old aviary.

There was a retired general—he said—

and he liked to run us like an infantry squad—and we did it, too, when we were in a particular mood.

"Beaks up, sparrows!" he'd bark. "We got a little girl on Fourth and Jefferson needs to catch a glimpse of her own mortality. Single file on the telephone lines. Sharpish! And not a peep out of any of you!"

Then we'd all perch silently on the wire, staring at whatever little girl got picked for a dose of memento mori, until she ran away. (Or threw rocks at us. Kids!) That's if we were in a particular mood. Other days a screeching flock in a dead tree was just what we needed—and it got the job done besides.

I told the general my routine about death once, right after a rain, when the ground was squirming with earthworms and we were all clean and full and cheerful.

"You can't even read your ticket until it's been punched," I said, woozy from rainwater and half my weight in worms. "That's the sticker. That's what makes dupes of us all. All these deaths out there, and they all belong to somebody else, right up until one of 'em picks you out and takes you home."

"That's pretty astute, soldier," he said. "Pretty astute. I'm going to recommend they promote you to crow."

Nothing came of it, of course; nobody's clout survives the grave. But it was a generous thought.

The aviary division was right up my alley. But winter came, and the flock flew south— the real flock, our temporary homes, the feathers that bore our little bellwethers of doom. Some of us stayed within the aviary, moving into barn owls, ravens, even (I hear) an albatross. Others scattered across the divisions like blown leaves. Mirrors. Spiders. Raindrops.

They gave me a shadow.

Shadows have rules. It's tricky work. I had to hitch rides under feet and in the undercarriages of cars and, when things were really dim, hunker between bricks, thinking sad jokes to myself about places the sun don't shine. Thing about shadows, though, is you can go anywhere you want—if you can get there—and I found myself slinking across the city, onto routes I'd known when I was living. Some I'd even forgotten. I slid from wall to shoe to tree and back again, winding through the city.

And there I was.

My corner.

Only it wasn't empty.

She was a breeze, flicking dried dandelion leaves between the cracks of the sidewalk. I huddled under them. She picked up a little, so that people held on to their hats.

"Ben," she said. "I should have guessed if I saw you again, it'd be here."

I couldn't say much. She was all around me, filling the air like her perfume used to do. Only she didn't need perfume to do it now.

"Remember how you used to say, 'death never calls to say it's coming?'" She'd bungled the line, but I held my tongue. "I think about that a lot. How I never expected it. Hit by a car! It's not as romantic as it sounds." She sighed, soft and low. "You were right about yours, though."

Whatever your family history, sometimes all it takes to trigger a heart attack is watching your true love smashed between a Buick and a building.

I said, "A breeze and a shadow. Pretty powerful omen. We oughta go into business together."

"Are you proposing?" she said, like she was smiling, like she still had something to smile with.

"Let's really own this death business," I said. "Make our own way. Together."

Turns out, it's never too late to really start living. But what do I know? I'm just an omen.

Amanda C. Davis is a combustion engineer who loves baking, gardening, and low-budget horror films. Her work has appeared or is upcoming in *Goblin Fruit*, *InterGalactic Medicine Show*, and *Cemetery Dance*, among others. Her collection, *Wolves and Witches: A Fairy Tale Collection*, co-authored with Megan Engelhardt, is available through **World Weaver Press**. She tweets enthusiastically as @davisac1. You can find out more about her and read more of her work at www.amandacdavis.com.

Holiday Recollection

THE SCARIEST HOLIDAY

by C.W. LaSart

Ah, Valentine's Day! The time of love and flowers, chocolates and cherubs shooting tiny arrows of lust into the rumps of unsuspecting lovers, and monstrous murderers hacking up young virgins! Wait. What? What do you mean there are no monsters on Valentine's Day?

I'm often bewildered by how little attention Valentine's Day gets amongst horror fans. I mean, sure, we have our token efforts like My Bloody Valentine and—shit! I can't think of any others, can you? Even Christmas has more horror movies dedicated to it than Valentine's Day. Forget about Halloween, that's too easy. So why is Valentine's Day so snubbed when it comes to horror? It is a proven fact that men who want to get action on that much anticipated third date often choose horror movies in lieu of romantic comedy. It's a no-brainer. Scare her and she'll snuggle right up to you. Get the adrenaline flowing and all kinds of good things can happen.

So why don't we think of horror when someone mentions February 14th? Think about it, what's more horrifying than love? Sex and horror are age-old friends. There are few things scarier than the physical act of love. The vulnerability, both emotional and physical (you are naked after all). The complete trust in someone else who you may barely know (in fact, may have just met earlier at the bar after a night of crappy karaoke and too much tequila). The potential for humiliation is staggering. And how about later? You may actually sleep next to this person. What if they're a whacko? What if you wake up in the middle of the night and open your eyes only to find their face a few inches from your own? Their teeth shining in the moonlight, drool dripping out of the corner of their smiling mouth to land on your pillow? What if you accidentally fart in your sleep? Spooky!

As horror fans, I propose we make a conscious effort to claim Valentine's Day as our own. Do something creepy each February.

Wear a hockey mask to work, or decorate your desk with the bones of small animals. As a divorced woman, my favorite Valentine's Day gift came the first year my Beloved and I knew each other. He went the traditional route of chocolates and roses, but he included one small token of appreciation that spoke directly of our twisted love for one another. After much searching on the Internet, he gifted me with an anatomically correct (and surprisingly life-sized), cherry-flavored gummy human heart. It was the sweetest thing anyone has ever given me. I knew then that he was a keeper, and seven years later, I know that I was right.

So I challenge you guys and gals, go that extra mile each year and make it a horror-themed Valentine's Day. Find your Beloved a realistic gummy heart, and if you can't, a real one will do in a pinch. Not nearly as tasty, but it's the thought that counts. Sure, they may think you're a freak, and then you'll have to go through that whole restraining-order business again, but you may just find that you are in love with a kindred spirit. Besides, if the person you love is the uptight, judgmental sort, isn't it really better to find out early? Before Halloween rolls around and they find out what you're really like?

Broken Beneath the Paperweight of Your Ghosts

by Damien Angelica Walters

Jacob sat alone with his brown paper heart in his hands.

He flexed his fingers, and the paper crinkled in response, a well-worn crinkle both familiar and frightening. The edges were tattered, the resemblance to old lace uncanny, and the names written on its surface gave it weight, substance. So many names. So many loves. All holding heartbreak within the lines and curves. He'd been careless for a long time.

He thought he'd been careful with Alexa. He thought he'd done everything right this time, yet she was gone now, too.

He hadn't moved since she closed the door behind her. Not a slam, but a quiet little click and, somehow, that made it far worse. He'd expected a slam. There'd been no parting kiss. No shouting. Nothing more than a sad half-smile and the words *I wish*.

"I wish..." he'd whispered, after the door closed.

But wishing was for children and fountains, for dreamers, for the dying in need of a miracle.

He traced Alexa's name with his fingertip. The graphite smeared across the paper and left trace of grey on his skin. Like a ghost of what they could've been.

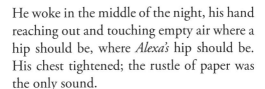

He woke in the middle of the night, his hand reaching out and touching empty air where a hip should be, where *Alexa's* hip should be. His chest tightened; the rustle of paper was the only sound.

One long strand of auburn hair lay coiled on Alexa's pillow. He wrapped it around his wrist, laced his fingers together behind his head, and stared at the ceiling. When tears stung his eyes, he blinked them away, rolled on his side, and breathed in the smell of her still clinging to the sheets.

Viv wrote her name in orange crayon. She had eyes filled with laughter and lips dancing with ideas.

"Let's go to Europe," she said one night.

"On vacation?"

"No, let's pack all our things and move."

"Just leave?"

"Yes. We could buy tickets tonight."

"I can't do that. I can't just leave my job, my family."

She crossed her arms over her chest. "Why not? You could get a new job and you can always come back to visit your family."

In the end, the lure of Europe was stronger than her affection. He found out when he called to ask if she wanted red or white wine with dinner. She laughed and said she was at the airport and she'd send him a postcard.

But she never did.

Some of the wax crayon had fallen off in tiny flakes, but the outline of her name was clear.

Three months after he and Alexa started dating, he showed her his heart. She said nothing. Cocked one eyebrow. Pursed her lips. He handed her a ball point pen but she simply twirled it in her fingers before she shook her head.

"No."

"I don't understand."

"I don't want to be another name."

"Okay, I understand," he said as he put away the pen, but he lied. He didn't understand at all.

Alexa moved into his apartment a year later and they celebrated with champagne and strawberries. He pulled out a fountain pen with a heavy, ornately carved barrel, the reservoir filled with ink of the deepest indigo, a shade that complemented the blue of her eyes.

"Please," he said.

"Jacob, I thought you said what we have is different."

"It is. It's real, it's perfect."

"Then I don't need to do that," she said, nodding toward the pen.

He twisted his hands together. The

words *but I need it* lingered on his tongue, but he swallowed them down.

❤

Karen scrawled her name with a waterproof marker. "So you won't ever forget me."

She liked to bite his lower lip when they kissed, sometimes hard enough to draw blood. She left scratches on his back when they fucked. She didn't believe in making love.

When they fought, which was often, she threw pillows, books, and once, a vase that split open the skin above his eyebrow, but when she whispered "I love you" and held his gaze, he felt himself drowning in the dark depths of her eyes.

He found out he wasn't the only one on a rainy Sunday afternoon when he visited her apartment to surprise her with sushi.

"Why?" he asked.

She shrugged and shut the door in his face.

Her signature was as sharp and clear as the day she wrote it.

❤

He tried leaving his heart out on the kitchen

table or the coffee table, always with a pen nearby. Alexa never said anything, but she didn't write her name, either. Then one morning, she came into the bedroom, holding his heart in the palm of one hand. He'd left it on the edge of the bathroom sink; she hadn't even moved it to wash her face and water droplets darkened one edge.

"You have to stop this, Jacob."

"I don't understand why you won't—"

"I'm not like them."

"I know you're not."

"Then you have to let this go. You have to let *them* go."

"What do you mean?"

"They're all still with you, all the time. It isn't healthy. Let it all go. For me, for us, but mostly, for *you*."

He found a scarf in the closet, tucked in the back, and a tube of lipstick in the medicine cabinet—Alexa's favorite shade of dusky pink. He called her cell phone but when her voicemail message began, her voice sent his heart skittering through the air and he hung up. An hour later, he dialed her number again and left a message.

"It's me. I found some of your things. I thought maybe we could meet for coffee and I could give them to you. Maybe we could talk, too."

While he spoke, he held one hand over his heart to keep it still.

Lila used red lipstick. She laughed all the while, her L's large and looping, and after, she kissed him until both their mouths were rose red and swollen.

They held hands even when they went out together to check the mail; they slept with their feet tangled up beneath the covers; they finished each other's sentences.

Until the day she stopped answering his phone calls. Even now, he didn't know what went wrong.

He finally wrote Alexa's name himself one night while she slept. It was impulsive, but it felt right. Comfortable. When she saw it, her eyes widened and one hand fluttered to her chest like a butterfly's wing.

"What did you do? Why? I told you I didn't want to be like that. I didn't want to be one of them. I'm *not* one of them."

"No, you're not like them at all. I'm sorry, I'll erase it if you want. I used a pencil." He smiled.

Her mouth opened. Closed. Opened again. When she spoke, her voice was little more than a whisper. "That's even worse. It's like a tattoo done with disappearing ink."

"But I love you."

"Do you?"

"Of course I do. How can you even ask that?"

He reached for her; she pulled away, her eyes sad.

Alexa returned his call after several days. "Can you just leave my things by the front door? I'll stop by and pick them up on my way home from work."

"Please, just meet me for one coffee."

She sighed heavily into the phone. "Jacob, I don't think that's a good idea."

He heard a muted voice in the background—her friend Maggie. He wasn't surprised she'd gone to stay with her; they'd been friends since college.

"Please, Alexa. Just one coffee."

There was a long pause and he curled his fingers around his heart.

"All right, fine. One coffee."

When she hung up, he couldn't help the smile that spread across his face.

Natalie used an old fashioned feather pen dipped into a pot of ink. Her letters were ornate. Delicate.

When she spoke, her words were often barely above a whisper and she had a careful measured way of walking, as if holding in some unseen hurt. He tried to convince her to talk about it, but she refused, telling him some doors were best unopened.

She slipped her hand free of his one night while they were walking beside the river. He heard a splash and waited until she emerged on the other side. She didn't wave or even bother to look in his direction, simply shook the water from her hair and walked away.

Jacob arrived at the cafe early and took a table in the back, setting the bag of Alexa's things on an extra chair. He'd packed everything except the scarf because he couldn't bear to part with it yet. Maybe when the smell of her had faded from the fabric...

When Alexa arrived, she hesitated before sitting down with her hands held tightly together. Silence and the smell of coffee hung in the air between them. Alexa was the first one to speak.

"Thank you for gathering up my things."

"You're welcome."

She shifted in her seat. Twisted her fingers together. And when she spoke again, her voice was small, soft. "I wish things could've been different. I really do."

"But I don't understand. You were happy, weren't you? Didn't I make you happy?"

"Yes, I was, but things changed after you wrote my name. *You* changed. Everyone gets their heart broken," she said. "You move on, everyone does. Everyone but you. You've kept it all inside like a memorial, like a trophy."

He leaned forward, over the table. "But it's the only way I can hold onto them."

"But that's just it. They're gone, they're all gone. You don't need to hold onto them, and while you were holding onto them, you were letting go of me."

"No, I wasn't. I swear I wasn't. Please, I'll try harder. I'll do whatever you want me to do."

"If you expect everyone to leave, you never let them in, and worse, you push them away until they have no choice *but* to leave." Tears shimmered in her eyes as she pushed her chair back from the table and stood up with her shoulders slumped. "Every time I looked at my name, I knew you were waiting for me to say goodbye. Don't you understand? I thought I was more than just a name, just a goodbye waiting to happen."

Her words were tiny barbs digging into the marrow of his soul. He didn't know what to say. He didn't know how to make it right.

She wiped tears from her cheeks, shook her head, and walked away, leaving the bag behind. The strength to call her back, to follow, hid beneath his pain, so he sat in silence, fighting tears.

Jenny, his first, used fruit flavored lip gloss. She didn't write her name; instead she pressed her lips gently against the paper, leaving an oily outline. When he closed his eyes, he could still taste the strawberries of her kiss.

They met in June at the beach—held hands, pressed footprints into the wet sand, and watched the waves rush in and out. And when the moon was full in the sky, their love rushed in and out, too.

At season's end, he said "I love you" and she promised to keep in touch.

A promise she didn't keep.

He took an eraser and worked slowly, carefully, so as not to tear the paper. He started with the last letter of Alexa's name and worked his way left, pausing here and there to brush the shavings off. When he was finished, there were slight depressions in the paper and nothing more.

He tried to erase the others, but he couldn't. It had been far too long; their names were firmly etched into the paper. He put his head in his hands and let his sorrow fall.

He picked up Alexa's scarf and breathed in her smell. He found more strands of hair caught on the sofa cushions and in the wood slats of the kitchen chairs, an empty shampoo bottle in the bathroom trashcan, and a coffee mug she'd bought him for his birthday. Every trace of her served only as a reminder that she was gone.

He stalked through the apartment, alternating between tears and anger. The weight of the names he could not erase turned every step into a heavy thud. The memories crowded and shoved, trying to bury Alexa's beneath theirs, but he wouldn't let it end like this. He couldn't.

In the drawer of his desk, he found a

permanent marker with a wide felt tip. He sat down with his heart, took a deep breath, and dragged the marker across the paper, partially covering Jenny's lip print. Pain, like a strip of skin being peeled free, bloomed in his chest and left him gasping for air.

Clenching his jaw, he returned the marker to the paper. The pain grew stronger with each new line. Even after he'd covered the entire print, a hint of sheen remained. He pressed harder, moving the marker back and forth, back and forth. Black bled through the paper, but eventually the gloss was covered.

He paused, breathing hard, then tackled the next name. The pain burned hot and bright, but he didn't stop until the name was covered. And the next and the next. The orange crayon and Lila's lipstick stubbornly resisted, and his fingers ached with the effort as he dug the felt tip in and scrawled over and over and over until they, too, vanished beneath a messy blob of black.

Finished, he dropped the pen and sat with his shoulders hunched. His breath rasped in and out of his lungs, an ancient locomotive straining to make it uphill.

When he finally lifted his heart, the paper tore, bits stuck to the top of the desk, and the ragged edges crumpled and fell off. He was left with a misshapen scrap filled with holes, but there was a bare spot in the center, a spot with the impression of Alexa's name.

The hurt in his chest subsided; the ache in his hands did the same. He held the ugly, battered thing that had been his heart in the palm of his hand, marveling at the change in its weight.

Now Alexa would know how much she'd meant to him. How much he wanted, needed, her in his life and how wrong he'd been about needing the others, and when she saw what he'd done for her, he knew she'd give him another chance. She had to.

Writing as **Damien Walters Grintalis**, Damien's short fiction has appeared in *Lightspeed*, *Strange Horizons*, *Interzone*, *Daily Science Fiction*, and others. Her debut novel, *Ink*, was released in 2012. As **Damien**

Angelica Walters, her work has appeared or is forthcoming in *Apex*, *Shimmer*, *Strange Horizons*, *Daily Science Fiction*, *Nightmare*, *Drabblecast*, *Pseudopod*, and the anthologies *Glitter & Mayhem* and *What Fates Impose*. A collection of her short fiction will be released in spring 2014 from **Apex Publications**.

HOLIDAY RECOLLECTION

EVERYTHING'S JUST METHADONE AND I LIKE IT

by Violet LeVoit

He was twenty-two, a skinny buck-thirty on storky five-eleven legs. Fat guys hate thin guys because thin guys are all cock. It's true. High cheekbones, green eyes, fangy grin. Hairless as a leather couch. I was thirty-six, a separated single mom. He cut through the haze of my domesticated malaise. He was the vampire ectomorph anarchist of my dreams, Johnny Rotten on a road bike. Fucking him made me see stars.

We're not together anymore.

There's not many twenty-first century ways for women to be ruined. Virginity only matters for royal brides, stretch marks are MILFed away, divorcees retire poolside with zinfandel, and rape victims bravely go public. There's no sinkhole, no shattered feminine Siberia where a careless slattern like you clutches her lace handkerchief and ponders her grim future as a Fallen Women. You curdle milk now, witch. The plague hand creeping under your corset, your cunt in its cold palm. I loved him so hard and so fierce my body made milk for him.

"You should go on dates," well-meaning people tell me. "Not some dumb kid this time. Someone mature. You know, there's a lot of divorced men who'd be happy to have dinner with someone as pretty and intelligent as you." I smile at them, politely. Colette said, "If I can't have too many truffles, I don't want any truffles." Everything's just methadone once you've had a wish made flesh.

Now I'm ruined.

He ruined me.

I'm fallen like Lucifer.

I go on dates. I have sex. But I know where I'm broken. I like it. The maimed fetishists in J.G. Ballard's *Crash* loved the snap of bone, the dizzy smell of spilling gasoline. I know how they feel. Seeing his name again, remembering the phantom sinew of his body against me, poking the abscess where our future used to be is like running from the wreckage. The doom of that statement thrills me. It might be better than being in love.

I clutch my handkerchief. I spill milk. I shiver, right in the pussy.

Holiday Recollection

THE SICKEST LOVE IS DENIAL

by Richard Thomas

In some ways, isn't love a sickness? It washes over you like a virus, making you sweat, as you lie awake at night—it alters your senses, makes your heart rattle the inside of your rib-cage like two birds fighting for the last worm, it makes you dizzy, and sends you out into the night, stumbling around, lost.

She was just a girl, somebody bent over a pool table, always grinning, that hint of cleavage, that Cheshire grin when her boy-friend left the room, dark doe eyes and long lush hair. If she cheated on him with me, then what could I expect but despair?

In the beginning it was long nights under the covers, every slick bit of flesh covered with my hands, my tongue, the world slipping away as we became the only souls left on the planet—floating on clouds, above it all. It was the only thing that mattered.

Eventually we moved in together, passionate and young, willing to live in the moment, to hide from the jealousies, the state of possession. Why not bring home a willing third wheel? How could it go wrong? Music and cold beer, then teeth on necks, long fingernails dragging trenches in my back, this is what all men wanted, more of it all, gasping and moaning, until the sun limped into the sky.

But then she started working late, coming home smelling of other women, strange perfumes, other men, their musk, and it turned my innards to knots. The long slow drag of a razor blade on my wrist as I waited for her to appear, waited for just enough strength to push a little harder, and then she was at my side, taking it away, kissing my bloody skin, licking, crying—never again, always mine, it would be okay.

And I believed her.

And then I stepped out myself.

Lost in the chaos, suddenly I was attractive, the lost bride on the last night of her freedom, the adventurous foreign exchange student, whatever my excuses, they were just that.

She would make me undress, this girl I loved, and sniff me from head to toe, asking me where I'd been, what was this bruise, this indentation? Are these teeth marks, is this lipstick? Give me your hand, your fingers— let me put them in my mouth.

It would only get worse. Pictures were taken, lines of powder, tabs of liquid gold, needles and days that never happened, and the freedom turned to violence to blood-stained sheets, and a stomach covered in bite marks that would take a week to heal.

There was a pregnancy.

Was.

Too damaged, no longer able to sustain eye contact, no longer able to keep the lies buried, this love turned sour, became our un-doing, required us to flee, to run in different directions, as fast and as long as we could.

It couldn't have ended any other way.

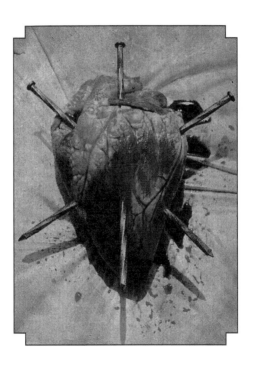

The Man of Her Dreams

by Tim Waggoner

Kristen was sipping a Singapore sling and trying to come up with an excuse that would enable her to leave as gracefully as possible when Barry walked into the bar. Oddly, she wasn't surprised, though she supposed she should have been. After all, until that moment Barry had existed solely in her dreams. But it seemed the most natural thing in the world for him to be here, weaving through the crowd, pushing past the drunken revelers from her office who had turned out to celebrate Lauren Foresca's promotion to regional sales manager, his gaze trained unwaveringly on her the entire way.

He stopped when he reached her table, nodded to the empty seat next to her. "May I?" His voice was the same mellow tenor that had spoken countless devotions to her while she slept.

She knew there was no possible way this

could be happening, that seven years as a sales rep for a textbook publishing company had finally taken their toll and her mind had snapped. Still, she smiled, gestured with her drink toward the chair. "Please."

He sat, moving with the fluid grace of a jungle cat. His eyes were the same deep blue as those of the Barry who inhabited her dreams, his hair the same blonde, so bright it nearly sparkled even in the bar's dim lighting. Mustache neatly trimmed, no sign of beard stubble even though it was 6:45. His facial features were at once both rugged and sensitive, so much so that he could have been a cover model for the romance novels Kristen devoured so eagerly. He wore a light gray shirt, dark gray khaki pants and freshly shined shoes.

"I bet you didn't expect to see me tonight." He smiled, displaying straight, even teeth so white they nearly gleamed. "Before you went to sleep, that is."

Before Kristen could reply, Lauren came walking unsteadily toward them, rum and Coke sloshing over the side of her glass. "You've been awfully antisocial tonight,

Kristen. One might get the impression that you aren't exactly thrilled by my promotion."

Kristen hated Lauren. Hated her grating, brittle personality, her love of office politics—the dirtier, the better—the way she looked like she was in her mid-twenties even though she was pushing forty, hated the low-cut mini-dresses she favored. Right then she especially hated the way Lauren didn't take her eyes off Barry as she spoke, the way she leaned forward to display her cleavage.

"Sorry," Kristen said, doing her best to keep the venom out of her voice. "I'm not much of a party person, I guess." *Especially when the party's for you*, she thought.

"That's all right. You can make up for it by introducing me to your handsome friend here." Lauren flashed Barry a smile which said *I'm extremely available.*

"I'm Barry." He reached across the table and enfolded Kristen's hand in a grip of velvet-wrapped steel. "Kristen's fiancé."

Lauren looked as if she had just swallowed a very large and juicy bug. "Really?" She turned to Kristen, her voice suddenly cooler by several degrees. "This is the first I've heard about it."

"I proposed to her last night," Barry said, smiling. "In bed."

Lauren looked as if she might bring the bug back up. "How very nice for you both." She gave Barry an appraising look, and Kristen knew what she was thinking: *How did a loser like you end up with a hunk like him?* "I suppose congratulations are in order."

"Thank you," Barry said. "Now why don't you go away and leave us alone?"

Lauren gaped. She was not used to being spoken to like that, especially by men. They usually fell all over themselves trying to please her in hopes of getting a close-up view of that cleavage. Kristen bit her lip to suppress a giggle.

Lauren scowled. "Now listen here Mr. *Fiancé*, I don't care who you are or what sort of brain damage you've incurred that's so obviously impaired your romantic judgment. But if you think for one minute—"

Barry stood and grabbed Lauren by the shoulders. He squeezed and she grimaced. She dropped her drink. It fell to the floor and shattered in a shower of glass and caramel-colored liquid.

The bar grew quiet; everyone turned to watch.

"Perhaps you didn't understand. I asked you to leave us alone." Barry's voice rumbled with barely restrained anger. "And I don't appreciate anyone making disparaging comments about my Kristen. Especially not a syphilitic tramp like you." Barry released her, walked over to Kristen and held out his hand. "Shall we?"

Kristen knew she would undoubtedly pay for this later at the office, but right now, she was delighted. Grinning, she took Barry's hand. "Let's."

He helped her up and together they left the bar, all eyes upon them, people whispering as they passed. It was an exit right out of a girl's dreams.

Kristen woke to yummy smells drifting in from the kitchen. She stretched and yawned, exhausted but contented. No, not merely contented—elated.

Last night had been beyond beyond.

After escorting her from the bar, Barry led them to Kristen's car and, at his direction, she drove them all over town on a night of unequaled romantic perfection.

First, Barry had her drive downtown, where they waded barefoot in a fountain. Kristen had always wanted to do that; it looked like so much fun when people did it on TV or in the movies. But she'd always been too afraid of being caught.

But not last night. Barry removed her shoes, set them neatly on the fountain's edge, lifted her as though she weighed little more than dandelion fluff (though her scale at home told a different story). He then lowered her into the water as gently as if he were placing a rose in a vase. She waded tentatively at first, then grew bolder. Finally, they were splashing and kicking water at each other like children. And just like in a movie, a police car came cruising by and they got out of the fountain quickly, laughing as they drove away in bare wet feet.

Barry then told her to drive to the small airfield on the outskirts of town. They parked where they could see the runway and watched planes taking off and landing, car windows rolled down so they could hear the throaty rumble of the engines. They wondered aloud at the identities of the pilots and passengers, who they were, where they were going or where they had been. Kristen was surprised at one point to look down and find herself holding Barry's hand. She didn't remember him taking it, but she didn't pull away.

After the airport, they drove to a park. The sun had set by then and the gate at the entrance was closed and locked. Barry was undeterred, though. He had Kristen pull over down the road a ways, and they climbed the fence and entered the park. Moonlight cast diamond-glitter on a small pond while bullfrogs and crickets called out to potential mates.

It was here, at the edge of the pond, water whispering encouragement, that Barry kissed her.

She knew all the clichés from her romance novels and from the movies every boyfriend she ever had referred to as "chick flicks." But the earth didn't move, her breath didn't catch in her throat, and he didn't touch the core of her womanhood in a way it had never been touched before. Barry's kiss did more than these things. It was as if the moment their lips touched she were made complete, a partial soul finally reunited with its missing half.

She lost no time getting Barry back to her apartment after that, and they made love. Barry had been considerate, thoughtful, attentive...so much so that he took care of her needs in lieu of his own. She lost track of how many orgasms she had. After the last time, he held her, stroked her gently, asked if she would stay awake with him and watch the sun rise. Unfortunately, that was the last thing Kristen remembered. She fell asleep.

But that was the only flaw in an otherwise absolutely perfect night, the best she had ever experienced in her life. And, unless her nose was wrong, it smelled like Barry was making breakfast. She wondered if he was as good at cooking as he was at everything else. Only one way to find out.

Even though Barry had explored every inch of her body quite thoroughly last night, she still put on her robe. Now that it was daylight, she was more than a little self-conscious about the extra weight she carried. She shuffled into the bathroom, peed, brushed her teeth, attempted to do something about her hair. Not that it helped; she still had a terrible case of bed head. Then she walked down the hall and into the kitchen.

Barry stood at the counter, dressed in the same outfit he wore last night. Kristen wondered if he even had any other clothes. His pants and shirt looked as if they had been freshly ironed, despite the fact that Kristen knew they had been tossed onto the bedroom floor last night. After all, she'd been the one doing the tossing.

Barry was busy chopping a green pepper with sure, deft motions. He'd already sliced an onion and a red pepper, their pieces collected neatly in separate wooden salad bowls. On the kitchen table, an omelet rested on a china plate, a sprig of parsley on the side. A cup of coffee and a glass of freshly squeezed orange juice completed the meal.

He looked up as she approached, smiled. "Good morning, Love. There's a ham and cheese omelet on the table waiting for you, and there'll be a western omelet, too, as soon as I finish chopping this pepper."

"Those are my two favorite breakfast dishes," Kristen said. "I can never decide between them."

"I know. But today you don't have to decide. You can have both." Barry returned to slicing the pepper.

Kristen felt a sudden hollowness in the pit of her stomach. "You really are Barry, aren't you? *The* Barry, the one from my dreams. That's how you know about the omelets, and that's how you knew I'd love all those things we did last night."

"Yes." He finished with the pepper and reached for an egg. He cracked it on the counter's edge and emptied it into a mixing bowl. He discarded the shell in the sink, then added the onions and peppers to the egg, humming as he stirred. He poured the mixture into the pan, and the omelet-to-be hissed and popped as it began to cook.

Kristen reached for her coffee with trembling fingers, lifted the cup, held it in two hands to keep it steady. "I guess I knew it all along. I mean, I recognized you when you walked into the bar." She took a sip of coffee. It was perfect: not too strong, not too weak, not too hot, not too cold. "But I really didn't think about what it meant. Everything happened so fast...I was swept along and didn't question what was happening or why it was happening. It was like—"

"A dream?" finished Barry. He lifted the pan off the burner, tilted it over a plate, and the omelet slid out easily. He set the pan back on the burner, turned it off, then placed the western omelet on the table next to the ham and cheese. Barry pulled the chair out for her, invited her to sit, and she did. He took the chair opposite her, and she noticed there was no plate for him, no coffee, no juice.

"Aren't you hungry?" she asked.

"I don't need to eat. You didn't dream me with an appetite." His smile held a hint of a leer. "Not for food, anyway."

She took another drink of coffee as she tried to gather her thoughts. "I've been dreaming about you ever since I was fourteen," she said finally.

"Thirteen," he corrected. "You were thirteen years, seven months and eight days old." She must have looked doubtful because he added, "A man doesn't forget his own birthday."

"I dream about you every night. Sometimes we ride horses in a meadow of flowing grass that ripples like the surface of a green ocean. Other times we go for long walks in an autumn wood, the leaves on the trees just beginning to turn colors. And as we stroll, we talk. No matter how trivial the topic I bring up, how silly I sound even to myself, you always listen, always make me feel like the most interesting person who ever lived."

"That's because to me, you are."

He had always been there for her, through a painful acne-scarred adolescence when boys wouldn't look at her, through college when the boys who asked her out did so only because they wanted to get into her pants, and on into an adulthood of diminished expectations—a boring job, disastrous dates, body beginning to sag, hair starting to gray. But none of that mattered when she went to sleep because Barry would be there waiting.

Except now he wasn't *there* anymore, was he? He was *here*.

"How is it possible? Dreams—literal dreams—don't just become real one day."

"They do if you need them to badly enough. You've dreamed about me every night for twenty-one years. Each night you invested a little more of your mental energy in me, until finally there was enough to allow me to cross over to your world."

Kristen frowned. "I just realized something. I didn't dream about you last night. Instead, I dreamed about..." She struggled to recall. "Trying to find a parking place at work. I drove for what seemed like hours, but all the spaces were filled, so all I could do was keep driving and looking." She grimaced. "It was so boring!"

"You didn't dream about me because I'm not in your head anymore." He spread his arms. "I'm here." He stood, came around the table, placed his hands on her shoulders and began massaging. "And I'm going to take care of you from now on."

Kristen thought she might melt under the warm pressure of Barry's hands.

"Now eat your eggs; they're getting cold."

Kristen picked up her fork, took a bite of the ham and cheese omelet, chewed while Barry continued kneading her shoulder muscles. She smiled. Maybe this *was* a dream come true after all.

"Aren't you supposed to be paying a visit on Adkins State?"

Kristen jerked awake and nearly fell out of her chair.

Lauren smirked. "Sorry to interrupt your nap."

Kristen turned in her chair to face Lauren, hoping she wouldn't comment on the haphazardly stacked reams of paper that cluttered the desk and floor of her cubicle. "I haven't been sleeping too well lately. I think I'm coming down with something."

Lauren took a half step back. "Whatever it is, don't give it to me. Now about Adkins State..."

"You're right, I was scheduled to visit the sociology department today." She rubbed her eyes. They felt sore and red. She hated to think how they looked; good thing there weren't any mirrors in her cubicle. "But I was feeling so lousy this morning that I decided to stay here and try to catch up on some paperwork."

Lauren glanced at the mountains of paper that threatened to take over Kristen's cubicle. "I can see you've made a lot of headway," she said in a sarcastic tone.

Kristen wished she could come up with a smart comeback, but her brain was tapioca. "I'll try to do better." Lauren had been on her case ever since that night over a month ago when Barry had insulted her. The last thing Kristen needed to do was give the woman any more reason to harass her.

"You certainly couldn't do much worse." Lauren turned to leave, then stopped. "By the way, how are things with you and Barry?"

Lauren's voice was neutral, but Kristen knew what game she was playing. She was hoping to find out that they'd broken up and Barry was available. Lauren was the kind of woman who wasn't turned off by a man insulting her. If anything, it made her even more determined to conquer him. Kristen started to say *Fine, everything's great, couldn't be better,* but the truth came out instead.

"Not so good."

"Really?" Lauren leaned forward, all attention.

Kristen didn't know why she was telling Lauren this. Maybe she needed to confide in someone, needed someone who would listen to her the way Barry used to in her dreams, even if that someone was an enemy.

"Do you think there's such a thing as a man who's too perfect?" Kristen asked.

Lauren laughed. "Honey, if there is, I sure haven't met him!"

"Barry does everything for me. He cooks all my meals, washes the dishes, does the laundry, cleans the apartment—including the bathroom—does the shopping, changes the oil in my car—"

"Good God, and you're complaining? Most women would kill for a man like that. I know I would."

"He insists on going out every night, and he always wants to do the same kinds of things—buy a bunch of balloons and set them free, go to a pet store to see the kittens, ride merry-go-rounds, sip wine by moonlight, take walks in the rain..."

"That all sounds very romantic," Lauren said wistfully.

"It is—the first few times you do it. But it starts to wear thin after a while. Sometimes I'd just like to stay home and relax, you know? And he doesn't talk to me; he just listens. He hangs on my every word as if it were a revelation from above."

"I've never had a man who listened to me like that." Lauren's voice was thick with envy.

"It's not the listening that gets to me. He never has anything to say—beyond talking about how wonderful I am, that is. He never has any thoughts or observations of his own to share."

"Some men aren't good at expressing themselves with words." Lauren paused, as if deciding if she should ask her next question. "What about the physical side of your relationship?"

"Boring. It's the same thing every night. He always wants to take care of 'my needs' instead of his own. Don't get me wrong, he's good at what he does, but would a little variety now and then hurt?" In addition, Barry had never climaxed during their lovemaking. Kristen wondered if he were physically capable of orgasm.

"Have you tried to talk to him about how you feel?"

"Of course. But he says he can't help it, that it's just the way he is."

"Then stay home. Tell him to sleep on the couch for a change."

"I've tried. But Barry can be quite... persistent when he wants something. He won't take no for an answer."

I can't help it, he'd said once. *I can only be what you've dreamed me to be.*

"Kristen, no offense, but you're certifiable. You've got what every woman fantasizes about, and all you can do is complain. Why don't you tell Barry to dump you and give me a call? I'd sure appreciate him." Lauren turned and walked off, shaking her head.

"I would if I thought it'd do any good," Kristen whispered. She hadn't told Lauren the worst part because there was no way the other woman would understand. In the few hours of sleep Kristen got each night, she still dreamed, but now instead of strolling through an autumnal wood with Barry, she dreamed of stupid, mundane things: trying to fit into jeans that were one size too small, walking along a sidewalk without making any forward progress, trying to read a book in which the letters were all jumbled nonsense. Her dream life with Barry had been her escape from reality, her refuge from the day-to-day banalities that everyone had to endure. But now that Barry had crossed over into the physical world, she had nowhere to escape to.

She couldn't go on like this. She was always exhausted, her work was suffering, and not only didn't she love Barry anymore— if she ever truly had—she was starting to actually hate him. Her dream had turned into a nightmare.

"Hi, Sweetheart. How was your day?"

The apartment was immaculate as usual.

Nothing out of place, no lint on the carpet, not so much as even a speck of dust on the furniture. The faint smell of cleaning chemicals in the air reminded Kristen of a hospital—antiseptic, sterile and cold. Barry puttered about in the kitchen, dressed in the same gray shirt and pants which never needed cleaning or pressing. She'd tried to get him to go out shopping for some new clothes (she was so sick of that damn gray!) but he'd politely refused.

"I'm making stir fry for dinner tonight. How's that sound?"

"Fine." She slumped wearily onto the couch. "Could you come in here for a minute? We need to talk."

Barry responded so quickly it was as if he'd materialized on the spot. "Yes, my love?"

She patted the cushion next to her. "Sit."

He did so, sitting with perfect posture, hands folded on his lap. He looked at her expectantly, his attention completely focused on her. Just once she'd like to see a hint of distraction in his expression—a glance off to the side to check what was on TV, a tightening of the lips as he fought to suppress a yawn.

She felt an urge to take his hands, decided against it. It was best to maintain some distance right now. "Barry, I'm afraid I'm not very happy."

His face clouded over. "What's wrong? Is it something at work? Don't tell me that bitch Lauren has been pestering you again." His hands curled into fists. "I'll go in with you tomorrow and tell her to back off."

"No! Uh, I mean, it's not work. It's...us." She sighed. "Actually, it's you."

"That's not possible," he said simply. "I'm everything you've ever wanted. I exist only to make you happy."

"There's such a thing as being *too* happy. Don't get me wrong, I appreciate everything you've done for me, but I need a little bit of mess and uncertainty in my life. Hell, I'd be happy just to get a good night's sleep for a change. You're smothering me with love and attention. Can't you understand that?"

He looked at her blankly.

Evidently not. She tried another approach. "I miss the way things were before you entered the real world. Isn't there some way you can go back to where you came from? Back into my dreams?"

Barry shook his head. "I may not be exactly human, but I am flesh and blood." He tapped his chest. "As long as I have corporeal existence, there's no going back. But I understand what's bothering you now, and I think I can fix it."

She smiled hopefully. "You do? You can?"

He nodded. "I haven't lived up to your expectations of me. I need to work harder to please you: keep the house cleaner, come up with more interesting things for us to do, be a better lover. From this moment on, Kristen, I will rededicate myself to your happiness. I will shower you with love such as no woman has ever known before!"

Kristen started to protest, but she knew it wouldn't do any good. "That sounds... wonderful."

He beamed. "I'm so glad we had this talk." He gave her a hug and a kiss on the cheek. "Now I really must get back to making dinner. I thought we might go wading in the fountain again tonight. We haven't done that for a while."

"No, we haven't." If four days counted as a while.

Barry returned to the kitchen, whistling tunelessly as he began chopping ingredients for the stir fry. Kristen closed her eyes and wondered what she was going to do. What if she told him point blank to get out? No, he'd probably just rededicate himself to making her happy all over again. She supposed she could not come home tomorrow. She could stay in a hotel for a while—days, weeks, if necessary—and wait to see if Barry left the apartment on his own. If not, she could always cancel her lease and let the apartment manager worry about throwing Barry out. But she doubted even that would get rid of him. He'd found her in the bar, hadn't he? What if there was some sort of connection between them which allowed him to hone in on her, to track her? If that were true, she'd never be rid of him. No matter how far she ran, eventually he'd find her, more determined than ever to make her happy.

She thought back to something Barry had said. *As long as I have corporeal existence, there's no going back.* She realized then what she had to do if she wanted to be free. She stood and walked into the kitchen. Barry was slicing a boneless chicken breast into bite-sized chunks on the cutting board.

"How about I help you with dinner tonight?" Kristen asked. "I know you like to do it all yourself, but if I help, we'll be finished and on our way to the fountain that much sooner."

"I don't know..."

"It would make me happy, Barry. Very happy."

"Well...all right." He smiled. "But just this once."

She nodded as she reached out and drew a long, sharp knife from the butcher block. "Once is all I need."

Three swift strokes later, it was finished. Barry lay on the floor, unmoving, eyes open and staring up at the ceiling. His shirt was torn, but no blood issued forth from his wounds. As Kristen watched, his form grew hazy and indistinct, until finally he evaporated like morning mist in the harsh glare of a summer sun.

That night, Kristen lay alone beneath her sheets.

"Forgive me?" she thought in her dream.

A pause, a sigh, a tolerant smile. *"Of course. I could never stay mad at you."*

Barry took her hand and led her toward a forest where the leaves were just beginning to turn gold and crimson.

It was perfect.

Tim Waggoner has published over thirty novels, three story collections, and his articles on writing have appeared in many publications. His latest horror novel is *The Way of All Flesh*, from **Samhain**. He teaches creative writing at Sinclair Community College and in Seton Hill University's MFA in Writing Popular Fiction program. Visit him on the web at www.timwaggoner.com.

Howling Through
the Keyhole

The stories behind the stories.

"Clocks"

I guess you can say "Clocks" is a story about haunting-by-detail. You can understand why, when a loved one dies, there is often a need to get rid of all their things, lest the memories continue to linger and there can be no closure. Here the memories do more than linger, and gradually recreate the past, which is why the protagonist finds the haunted place irresistible, despite his better judgment. So he is trapped by his own longing. The image of all the clocks linked together probably was suggested by an Outer Limits episode which had a similar arrangement, for turning back time if I remember correctly.

–Darrell Schweitzer

"Hearts of Women, Hearts of Men"

At the most basic level, I wanted to show how hollow the consumerism of Valentine's Day is compared to real emotions. I also wanted to step outside the box and show something other than just the love of a couple. It's okay to love and care for people we aren't in relationships with, and it's also okay to stand up for them.

The story went through several phases, and the end product is a far cry from the original premise. The killer was originally a man. When I told my wife the killer was going to be a woman instead, she first looked shocked, then angry. When asked why, she said the flip totally changed the scenario in her mind and that she was upset by that fact, that gender roles should influence her thought process to that degree (she's not one to go in for gender roles, and I applaud her for that).

Why is it more shocking when a woman kills a man, and what does this say about the content of the story? Are we, as a society, still more accepting of abuse toward specific groups of people?

Also, candy hearts taste like chalk.

—*Zachary C. Parker*

"Sauce"

I wrote "Sauce" after ten consecutive years of dysfunctional romantic relationships with two different men, both of which ended the exact same way. The first was my ex-husband and the second was a long-term boyfriend that I lived with for four years.

I think most people fall into patterns in their relationships, and I had a tendency to get involved with self-absorbed, immature men who were not looking for a partner to share intimacy with, but rather a mother figure that would take care of them. The issue with treating your girlfriend/wife like your mother is that they have needs and desires that get ignored, which creates resentment, dissatisfaction, and ultimately a desire to leave. I told people after my divorce was finalized that my ex-husband was less a mate and more of a houseplant that I needed to water once in a while. The problem with being married to a houseplant is that they don't clean up after themselves and they are terrible in bed.

With both relationships, I felt ignored, lonely, and sexually unfulfilled in a way that gnawed at me every single day. When I realized I'd fallen into another relationship that was the same as my marriage (and that fact truly took a while to set in), I broke it off and found myself a single lady once more, at 31 years old.

I told a good friend of mine, who later turned into my current partner, that I felt like both men emotionally erected a monument to me in their subconscious yard. They told me how beautiful and wonderful and *special* I was to them. I've heard countless times how I'm "the best thing that ever happened" to them. They tell me how they can't live without me, how I've made them complete. But then when it came down to the serious business, to building a life inside the house, there was no effort to build a future together and maintain whatever romantic love was there. After years of a one-sided effort, with no intimacy, there was nothing to show, and ultimately I ended up leaving both men and breaking their hearts. With this image in mind, I sat down and wrote "Sauce."

–*Catherine Grant*

"Silence"

This is a story that I've been meaning to write for nearly five years now. I've always been a sucker for guilt and the horribly haunting power of regret, not to mention having a deep interest in the themes of isolation and despair (I even edited an anthology based on just those themes). For whatever reason, the image came clear in my head: there would be a closeted gay man named David, a Vietnam vet stricken with ALS and nearing the end of his days, and he would be haunted by a demon that might or might not be real. I just knew it would be brilliant.

However, I could never actually get myself to write the damn thing. I had the outline all set, even going so far as to illustrate the demon's circuitous path through David's living room and how each object correlated to events in his past. And yet at the end of it all, it took *five freaking years* to actually sit down and write it. I've read quite a few stories where straight writers penned tales about gay characters that just didn't work at best or were downright insulting at worst. I wasn't confident in my ability to pull it off.

But why did I write it now, after all this time? Pretty much all because of Ken Wood. I'd written another short story for Shock Totem's first holiday issue a couple years back, and let's just say I was quite disappointed in what I'd written. So when Ken came to me asking if I'd like to be a part of this second holiday issue, I decided that what I presented needed to be exceptional, if only to make up for my past (self-perceived) failure.

And yet it *still* wouldn't have been written if not for Ken's prodding. I hemmed and hawed and bided my time, writing little bits here and there and then deleting what I'd written, thinking it crap. Finally, Ken wrote to me with a firm deadline. Two days. That's it. I promised I'd get him the story come hell or high water.

Lo and behold, I did it. All I had to do was stop thinking about how I wouldn't do the subject justice and write it, already. The first draft, nearly eight thousand words, was written in a single day (aided by my original, now-outdated outline), and subbed the next after going over the story with my wife. I knew it was good, perhaps nearing exceptional.

Yet still there was a lingering sense that there was something slightly off about it.

Here comes Ken again. He said he loved the story overall, and then pointed out to me *exactly* what was wrong—the ending. It sucked. Royally. We wrote back and forth a few times, trying to figure out how to make it better. In the end it was Ken who came up with the idea to have David slightly redeem himself, even if it was too little, too late. I was so excited, I couldn't fall asleep that night. The story was finished. Finally.

And so there you have it, a little bit of insight into the creation of this story, one I'm pretty damn proud of. No writer this side of Salinger can create in a vacuum. We're all the sum of the other creative individuals we know. They inspire us, they urge us on, they're our greatest supporters, and sometimes they can help you out of a self-made jam. I've been blessed with so many of them over the years, few more meaningful to me than Ken Wood. So thanks, Ken, for dragging this story out of me. I appreciate it a ton.

–*Robert J. Duperre*

"Golden Years"

I was watching an old couple bickering one day. It was obvious they had decades together under their belts and still loved each other. But the nagging and bickering was a bit funny. I just took it one sinister step further.

–*John Boden*

"She Cries"

The title "She Cries" has been with me for a long time. It's been the title of a poem, a song, and the name of a music project. When

I first wrote the story printed here in *Shock Totem*, "She Cries" struck me as the perfect title.

I can only speculate as to why these two words—*she cries*—have always resonated with me, but this is not the place to explore it.

So let's talk about the story.

Our lives are littered with the wreckage of past relationships. Most of us move on from one to the next, able to navigate our way free of the disappointment, the pain, the sadness. Some, however, carry that wreckage with them, from old relationship to new, afraid to let it all go, and ultimately perpetuating the cycle because of it. They're emotional hoarders, and as the years pass, the weight of it all begins to wear on their souls. At its core, this is what "She Cries" is about.

The idea was inspired in me many years ago after a night out with friends. We'd been drinking, and at the end of the night one of my oldest and dearest friends broke down in tears. She'd been through a long series of failed relationships and it was all beginning to pull her under. That night, she didn't want to be left alone. I remember her words distinctly: "I just want you to hold me. I want to feel safe."

This haunted me for a long time, because she'd peeled back the layers and had given me a glimpse of the twisted remains that littered her insides, and it hurt.

"She Cries" doesn't touch upon that moment specifically, but it does explore her psyche a bit in Anna Triste, a haunted woman who isn't strong enough to let go of the wreckage from her past and the sadness that controls and consumes her. Because of that, those who wish to help her, or truly care about her, or rely upon her, often find themselves hurt, heartbroken, or worse.

The metaphor probably isn't as clear to the reader because I know the history of and the catalyst for the story, but I'm confident it isn't necessary for one's enjoyment of the tale. At least I hope so.

As an aside, this story originally appeared in *Anthology: Year One*. I heavily updated it for this release. This is my preferred version.

–K. Allen Wood

"Omen"

Shock Totem hosts a flash-fiction contest every two months, which I am delighted to participate in whenever I can: I like seeing the prompt interpreted thirty different ways, and the "slush experience" of evaluating so many stories of the same length and theme. In January 2013, the prompt was a sad news item about a cystic fibrosis patient dying of cancer in her transplanted organ, which included the line: "She was dying a death that was meant for someone else." "Omen" was based (very loosely) on that prompt.

My goal in themed flash contests is to amuse myself, create as complete a story as possible, and incorporate the theme only close enough to keep from getting disqualified. (Not a recommended approach!) I got a kick out of it, anyway!

–Amanda C. Davis

"Broken Beneath the Paperweight of Your Ghosts"

I could say my story is metaphorical with the

paper and the names as a stand-in for the damage lovers leave behind, but I think I'd rather wish my protagonist well, tattered heart and all.

–*Damien Angelica Walters*

"The Man of Her Dreams"

"The Man of Her Dreams" was originally written for a DAW anthology titled *A Dangerous Magic*. The anthology's theme was, as the title suggests, fantasy romance stories with a dark edge. I thought about the wish-fulfillment aspect of category Romance fiction, and wondered what it would be like if someone really could conjure up their perfect lover. What would such a lover be like, and just how long could he or she remain "perfect?" "The Man of Her Dreams" is my attempt to answer those questions.

–*Tim Waggoner*

SILENT Q DESIGN

Silent Q Design was founded in Montreal in 2006 by **Mikio Murakami.** Melding together the use of both realistic templates and surreal imagery, Mikio's artistry proves, at first glance, that a passion for art still is alive, and that no musician, magazine, or venue should suffer from the same bland designs that have been re-hashed over and over.

Mikio's work has been commissioned both locally and internationally, by bands such as **Redemption, Synastry, Starkweather,** and **Epocholypse.** *Shock Totem #3* was his first book design project.

For more, visit **www.silentqdesign.net.**

ALSO AVAILABLE FROM SHOCK TOTEM PUBLICATIONS

CURIOUS TALES of the MACABRE and TWISTED

SHOCK TOTEM

LESLIANNE WILDER
RICARDO BARE • CATE GARDNER
VINCENT PENDERGAST • DAVID JACK BELL
GRÁ LINNAEA & SARAH DUNN
A conversation with James Newman • Nonfiction by Mercedes M. Yardley

SHOCK TOTEM MAGAZINE
Issue #2 – July 2010

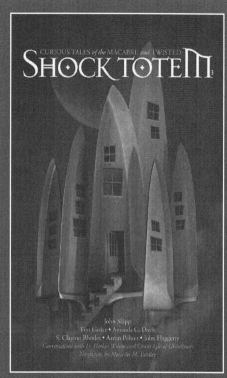

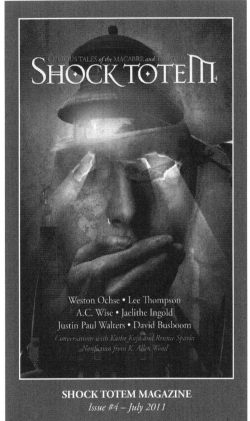

ALSO AVAILABLE FROM SHOCK TOTEM PUBLICATIONS

CURIOUS TALES *of the* MACABRE *and* TWISTED

SHOCK TOTEM

William F. Nolan • S. Clayton Rhodes
Amberle L. Husbands • Kristi DeMeester • M. Bennardo
Damien Angelica Walters • Victoria Jakes
Conversations with Laird Barron and Violet LeVoit
Nonfiction from Kurt Newton

SHOCK TOTEM MAGAZINE
Issue #7 – July 2013

AVAILABLE IN PRINT AND DIGITAL FORMATS
www.SHOCKTOTEM.com

ALSO AVAILABLE FROM SHOCK TOTEM PUBLICATIONS

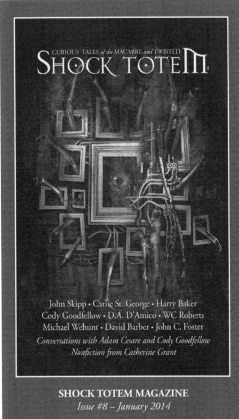

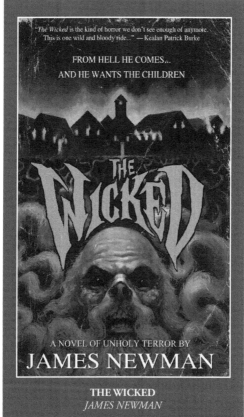

ALSO AVAILABLE FROM SHOCK TOTEM PUBLICATIONS

DOMINOES
JOHN BODEN

FIND US ONLINE

http://www.shocktotem.com

http://www.twitter.com/shocktotem

http://www.facebook.com/shocktotem

http://www.youtube.com/
shocktotemmag

Made in the USA
San Bernardino, CA
25 January 2015